Poveglia's Plague Doctor

Emilia Voortman

Poveglia's Plague Doctor

DB

First print 2024
Author: Emilia Voortman
Coverdesign: Emilia Voortman
ISBN: 9789083399249
NUR: 330
© 2024 Emilia Voortman
Published by: Donkey Books | www.donkey-books.com

Mijn eerste pannenkoek

PROLOGUE

"Servius Piscius Festus" was written on a little chalk sign that hung to the right of an old hospital bed. The sign was slightly tilted. Names, that had been written on it before, were still slightly visible. A hideous sign. I stood with trembling legs at the end of the hospital bed, tilting my head so the sign would be straight. Every muscle in my body was tensed. I had never imagined that I would write the name of my own master on one of them. But when his time came my shaking hands managed to get his name down. The fingertips of my glove were stained white by the chalk. I brushed them off on my black cloak, which only made the stain worse. Servius had helped so many people, but now there was no one that could help him. I had been terrified when Servius had begun to show signs of the plague. I had tried everything I could to prevent him from dying, but there had been no use to it. He has been coughing up blood for days, he is sweaty, tired and slender. Servius had slowly been dying and now his end is near.

CHAPTER 1

The sun was shining through the windows behind the hospital beds. I imagined that the warmth from the sun was like a pleasant hug to the people who were dying. The warmth could have made them think about someone they loved. Someone they lost. Someone about to lose them.

It had just turned afternoon and the sound of the ringing bells in the belfry washed over the entire island. The bells were the only indication of time there was on Poveglia. Time didn't matter here. People needed help when they needed help. I sometimes question why we even use the belfry. Then I am reminded of the many ships that pass our little home.

The silence returned just as I sat down on a chair beside Servius's bed. 'Fransisco.' he said. He was having trouble breathing and he seemed even worse than before. He was so close to dying, but I was nowhere near saying goodbye to him.

'Yes, master.' I said, my knees touching the cold stone ground as I kneeled beside him. Desperate to hear what he was going to say. My fingers followed the frame of the hospital bed. Touching the deckled edges of where the paint had begun to disappear. Most of the paint was already peeled off and was showing what was beneath. There was a gasping for air.

'You need to do something for me.' Servius said. He took a deep hoarse breath. I had never dared see him like this. I had known him for my entire life. He was like a second father to me. My own father had worked alongside Servius up until a few years ago. The plague had caught and killed him. But although he had died, things hadn't changed much. Servius was still there and had always been the head of the island. I never asked how he became the head of the island. He had a leading nature. He handled Poveglia just fine. So fine that he even had the time to be my teacher; although that only happened late in the evenings. Or a rare day on which he had time to spare. He had taught me most things I now know; Italian, French, Latin, geography and astronomy.

Servius closed his eyes and reopened them. The twinkle in his eyes was gone. He looked at me with a dull gaze, as if to say "I'm not really here". A body left behind by its soul.

'I'm going to die Fransisco.' He said. My mouth was shut tight. Not letting me speak, imprisoning the hope inside me. False hope. I wanted to shout at him to keep fighting, that he wasn't done yet. That he couldn't leave me now. 'I assume you already knew that. Set aside you've come to terms with it.' A slight cough, that sounded more like he was choking, escaped his mouth before he continued. 'When I'm gone, and when this plague is gone, I need you to do something for me.' He weakly raised his hand. Slowly taking off his glove. I didn't dare to intervene even as I saw how much he was struggling. Beneath the glove his thin fingers were black. He took off the ring that was placed on his ring finger. The ring almost fell off, as the ring was too big for him. It was a silver ring. It was big enough to carry an engraving on it. I had never inspected this ring before, as Servius was very protective of it. He was protective of most of his stuff. 'When I die, I want you to take this ring. You must keep it safe, on your finger underneath your glove; at all times. You must not show it to anybody. You will burn me. You will take my ash. You must bring both to my wife. Do you understand me?' His voice was stern. I nodded. That was all I could do. My body was frozen into place. He grabbed my hand with incredible force. 'I need to hear you say it.'

'Yes.' I said, my voice small. 'Yes, master.'. The grip around my hand loosened as his hand slipped away. He put his ring back on his hand which he hid under the glove. He leaned back, falling asleep before his head could hit the pillow. The silence felt most uneasy to me as I stayed kneeled down beside him. His breathing slowed down. My heart skipped a beat every time he stopped his breathing for a second. I stood up, fearing to see him die in front of me. My knees were aching as I walked out of the infirmary.

Before my master was placed in the infirmary I had barely spend time here. My master used to keep me away from it. Saying that it was no use being here. Most of the people that were placed here were doomed to die. They were put on the infirmary on the western side of the island; away from the others. The only times I visited, before Servius was placed here, was when someone dead had to be moved. It was a job nobody wanted, but had to be done. Servius had made it my job. I was fully in charge of where the people went after they had died. Luckily the route was already planned out.

I have seen many corpses. The first time I ever saw one was when I was eleven. My father had tried to keep me away from all the infirmaries. I had spent most of my younger years in the housing, kitchen, church or by the water. Little by little Servius took me to more places on the island and before I knew it I was working alongside him.

My father had protested when Servius took me into the infirmary. But Servius is stubborn, and he knew that. Servius told me that it was about time that I saw what death was. He wanted me to be comfortable with the idea of an end. In a way I think that he was preparing me for this moment. The moment I would have to say goodbye to him.

The front doors were open and there was a slight wind finding its way between the leaves of the trees, but it didn't reach my face. It was late summer but the days were hotter than ever. The black suit and the plague mask that I needed to wear weren't helping much. My breath fogged up the glasses, making it hard to see.

Even though it wasn't nice to wear, I was glad I had it. It was supposed to keep me from getting sick. It had done so for my master for many years. And even though I now know that I can still get sick while wearing the mask, I still carry it with me everywhere I go. The mask gives me a comforting feeling. The mask is also supposed to keep away any bad smells. It has a little space for dried flowers and orange peels, but that doesn't really work. The dried flowers do nothing against the smell of dying people. A smell that dwelled over the entire island. It wasn't a nice smell, but it would always be better than the smell of burned bodies.

Now that I was outside, I took my mask off. My lungs were filling themselves with 'fresh' air. Even though I could still smell the scent of dying people, the salt from the sea overtook some of it. It felt nice to be able to breathe. I felt alive. I wondered how many times Servius had felt like this. I imagined Servius standing in the evening sun, at the edge near the water. His eyes locked on the horizon, even if there wasn't anything to see in the distance. The times that I had sneaked after him, knowing that I shouldn't. Always looking at him, hidden from behind a tree. I had wondered what he was looking at, why he did what he did. later I joined him. He told me why he did it. To feel alive. Would he ever feel like that again?

'Sir?' A small voice came from behind me. I took another deep breath before turning around. The woman in front of me was Alice. She wasn't here to take care of people, she was here to find a cure. Her father had been working on it before her, but he had died. Alice wanted to stop the suffering and find the cure her father had been working on; so she stayed.

Servius had never liked her and I knew exactly why. Alice was shy but extremely stubborn, even more so than Servius himself. He didn't know how to handle that. I used to be close friends with Alice when I was younger. We had often made Servius angry. We grew more distant as we both had to work and time slipped away. It had changed a lot between us.

'You know you can still call me Fransisco, right?' Alice had red hair that glistened in the sunlight. Her hair normally reached to her hips. But was now bound in a shorter braid. Her eyes were dark brown and she wore a white dress that reached a little above her shoes. The bottom of it was slightly stained, but not enough for someone to call it dirty. She held her hands behind her body as she shifted her weight between her feet, her eyes meeting mine as she smiled. I couldn't help but smile back.

'Yes, sir… Fransisco, I mean.' She bowed her head down to the ground and shook her head. A small chuckle escaped her lips.

'What are you here for, Alice?'

'The men at the port wished to speak to you. They said that they have news. They wouldn't tell me what, but were too lazy to get you themselves.' It wasn't usual for me to be called up to the port. They were normally busy with checking the ships.

'I'm on it, thank you.' Alice gave a quick nod and ran off to the hospital. I walked off towards the sea; making my way to the port.

Poveglia isn't the largest island, but there is everything you may need. Maybe even more than that. Poveglia consists of three smaller islands combined. The burning grounds are placed on the most northern island. This is where all the dead people are burned and buried. Away from the main island south of that. There is a little wooden bridge between the islands that keeps them connected. The main island is where all the buildings are; with most of the people. There's a little church most doctors visit to pray. To pray that they won't get sick like the rest.

There's a cavana on the southern side, near the smallest island; it's an island doctors hardly ever visit. The boats come in that way, and that's the point where they get checked. All sick people must stay on the island, as the rest may continue their way towards Venice.

On the northern side of the main island is the hospital, together with the housing. The belfry and the kitchen are located there as well. There are a few more buildings scattered on the island, like the outhouse, and other parts of the hospital.

The wind rushed through my hair, along my neck into my suit. I watched as the waves hit the island as I walked past. I had a small urge to jump into the water. I had done so many times in the summer when I was little. I didn't care much about the stories back then.

Everyone in Venice talks about this island. Calling it "haunted". They believe that we throw the bodies of dead people into the sea. Many fisherman stay away from the island, scared that they will catch a corpse in their nets. They won't find any. The burning grounds are sufficient; for now. I wouldn't even think about dropping bodies in the sea. They were people too, after all. As a child, I didn't care what other people thought of me and just jumped in. A refreshment after a long day of work in the sun. Now that I'm head of Poveglia I can't do that anymore. It wouldn't look 'good' if the head of an island would swim in a sea, supposedly, filled with dead bodies. I'm considered weird enough already by working on the island. Few people are thankful, but even they don't get why I do it. Sometimes I wonder too, when I get eager to leave this world behind. I've fantasized about leaving Poveglia more times than I can count, but I never went through with it. I grew up here with a purpose, and I will see it through.

I arrived at the port, walking towards the five men who were standing next to one another in a small circle. They were all leaning a little forward, talking to one another. They couldn't be heard over the soft crashing of the waves.

'Morning.' I said rather as a question than a statement. Hoping it wasn't some cult meeting that I had just intervened. All eyes were fixed on me within an instant.

'Fransisco! Good morning, how are you?' one of the men said in a mocking voice.

'You wanted to see me?' I said, ignoring his question. I knew that it would annoy him. As expected his face displayed a look of disgust.

'Yes, it's about the ships.' he said in a low hum, not moving his lips. 'Less and less sick people are coming in. Most of them are healthy, if not having another sickness we can't cure.' he spit out while looking at the empty port.

'Well, that's great.'

'Yes it's amazing, but what are we to do?'. The men that were standing around him had reformed themselves into a neat row. Most of them had crossed their arms and were staring at me with a stern look. I straightened myself and held my gaze at the man whom I was talking to. 'We would have to inform the authority of Venice, tell them things are getting better. We need to know for how long we will have to keep checking the ships. When will we abandon thi-'

'Those are things for me to take care of. Your job is to keep track of the amount of sick people that come in. I'll do the rest. About when we can leave this island, I don't know yet. Only the future can tell us.' I interrupted him. The man in front of me shifted his weight between his legs. His face carried a grim look like he was weighing the options on how to bring me down.

'How will you do the rest if you don't know how to?' he said, as he got closer to me.

'What makes you think that I don't know how to?'

'I knew Servius. The way he talked about you. Ain't no way that he was a real doctor. They made a mistake by making you the head of the island.' I kept my face blank, showing no emotion. I knew what Servius would have done if he were in my place. That man wouldn't have walked off with the same ignorance he was wearing now. Servius was confident, he never let anyone walk over him in this way.

'Is.'

'What?' the man said lowering his head to my face.

'Servius is, not was.' I looked him dead in the eyes, as the man burst out in laughter. I don't have the confidence that Servius has. I'm not that strong. Even though I knew that it was wrong of him to talk to me in that way, I couldn't change it. Whatever I would say next, it wouldn't help. So I turned around and walked off.

'Well look at that.' the man said through his laughter. 'Go get your little master, like you always have. You aren't strong enough to do it on your own. You're his dog. Don't worry! It seems like he could use one; that weak old man!' the men behind him joined in his laughter. I stopped dead in my tracks. I held my head up a little higher as I turned around to meet his gaze. The man hadn't seen that coming. I made use of this and walked over to him in big strides. His confidence had disappeared for one second. Enough for me to grow mine. I only stopped when I was half a meter away from him. A little spark of fear arose in his eyes. A fear that I had seen in many others.

I grabbed the man by his shirt and without thinking dragged him to the waterside. The man made little noise and put all his effort into stopping me. My grip was too tight for him and before I knew it I had thrown the man into the water. There was a big splash, as some of the water hit my face. All the other men had gone quiet. The man arose waving his arms like crazy, water splashing everywhere. His face was filled with terror.

'Talk to me like that once more and I'll give you a dive into one of the burning pits.' I spoke clearly. There was a low murmuring behind me that I didn't take notice of. I looked down at the water, waiting for an answer. My reflection was there, black without any depth. Still, I could feel it looking back at me. The reflection didn't quite match me. For a moment it wasn't mine, but that of Servius. The little bit of him that lived in me.

The reflection became weary from the rippling water. The man had swum over to the side of the island and was desperately trying to raise himself onto it. He took quick glances to see if I would push him back in. I knew they were scared of the water. Even though he should know better than those made-up stories. The thought of it was enough to scare a grown man.

Deciding that I would let him go I turned around and started walking back towards the infirmary.

CHAPTER 2

News travels quickly. Especially when on a small island. It had not been more than half an hour later when I entered the infirmary for another time. From the moment I walked in all eyes were pointed to me. The doctors put down their work for a moment. It felt like I was looking at a picture of this moment rather than living in it. My eyes scanned the room but avoided making any eye contact with any of the doctors. My hands clutched by my side, my eyes made their way to Servius.

He lay still in his bed. The covers up to his chin, head resting on a stack of pillows. Mouth slightly open, breathing with great difficulty. The sudden silence had awoken him. His gloomy eyes now lit up when he saw me. There was no smile on his face, but the tiny spark in his eyes had more than enough meaning.

I quickly walked towards him, not wanting him to wait. I only noticed later that at that time I had a slight grin on my face. 'I heard about what you did.' Servius said, with less trouble speaking than he had before. For a moment I let myself believe that there was still a chance for him. A thought I knew was stupid; something I thought but not believed. But in that moment that didn't matter. I looked him in the eyes. Without fear of what he was going to say about it.

'I didn't mea-' I started but wasn't allowed to finish.

'Don't ruin it now. From what I've heard he deserved it. I never saw you for a man of such action, but then again, I taught you well!' there was a little silence. Servius took in a deep breath, wanting to say more, but I saw he could not. 'God, I would have wanted to see his face. Was he scared?'.

'Petrified.' Servius let out a small laugh; a real one. It made him glow up. I hadn't thought he was still capable of laughing. His muscles moved; strong ones that he had built up from the heavy work he had been doing his entire life.

'Keep doing this.' his eyes softened. 'Pushing people in the water I mean. Maybe it will make you feel like I'm with you.' His voice was low; exposing a different part of him. A deeper more personal part of him that he had done so much trouble for to keep hidden. He noticed some of the doctors were eavesdropping; who gave him questionable looks. 'But only when they deserve it, of course.' he said, giving me a quick wink. Servius had always made a bit of trouble. When someone disrespected him he made sure it wouldn't happen again. The same went for me, he wouldn't stand anyone disrespecting me.

Servius gave a stern look to one of the doctors, who quickly scurried away.

It sometimes felt like Poveglia was the only thing there was. Like there didn't exist a world beyond the island. At times it felt great. Worries of the world around, unable to reach you. But at other times it felt rather dull. A boring cycle of day after day; with no way of escaping. I knew those doctors who were listening to us felt the same.

'What if people think I act out of anger?' I whispered. Servius looked me in the eyes, taking a few seconds, carefully forming an answer.

'I know that as doctors we should have patience.' He started. I sat down next to his bed. Leaning forward, eager to hear him speak. 'But we too have emotions, which we do not always have control over. They do too. Remember that you are above them; you have a little power over them. I'm not saying that you should use that power just because you have it, but know that you can make a little trouble now and then. They shouldn't punish you for simply feeling. It won't hurt to take down a rumour or create them. God I wish I had used that power more.'

' What more would you have wanted to do?' I questioned. 'You have made quite the trouble.'

'Punish the wrong; of course!' Servius groaned. 'Or push them in the water. I know I've punished a lot of doctors, but doctors aren't the only people in the world who are wrong.' Servius began to cough, heaving for air in between. I held my handkerchief up to him. When he stopped couching I saw the blood on it and quickly folded it up to throw away.

'You wouldn't have been able to punish all wrong Servius. There is too much wrong for a single soul to eliminate.' I spoke softly.

'Oh, I know! But I had power. Everything was under my control once. I could have punished the wrong of an entire country, maybe even more. He lay down, I could see the strain it had taken him to talk. 'But someone else took over. Perhaps wanting to do the same, starting with me.'

'Poveglia does seem like its own country, I know.' I didn't want him to think I was making fun of him; or that I thought he was going crazy. Though sometimes I questioned if he wasn't all mad. I never spoke this thought out loud to anyone. Not daring all the whispers would take it back to him. Weird stuff happens when the mind gets tired. Poveglia had been a great place for the crazy. Some hear more, some hear less. Some think more some think less. Some speak, and never stop, while some have lost their voice. Servius told me this was all based on the person you were before. I often wondered if it wasn't the person you were, but the person you are. Only now visible because the person around it is no longer able to keep it hidden. Servius wasn't easy to place. He hadn't really changed. His body was tired, but his mind was still full of energy.

'That's not what I meant.' Servius said in a warning voice. I didn't know what he meant but didn't ask. He got that I wasn't going to say anything more. 'Trusting has never been your strong side.' Our eyes met, he took my hand. His voice was soft like he was scared to hurt me. Something that had only happened a handful of times. It had always scared me a little. The stern strong Servius had been the one I knew so well, the one that was always there. But when he changed like this all seemed a lot more serious. 'Keep it that way. This world is not to trust.'.

His grip around my hand weakened. 'I'm dying.' He whispered to me. Servius let out a small sigh. Eyes wide open, mouth closed. It had taken a while before I realised he was really dying at the moment. I quickly grabbed his hand. As to keep him from being taken away from me. That was the last sound Servius would ever make. Forever to be burned into my memory. The silence in him returned once more and this time it wouldn't go away. I held his hand. Hoping that he was still breathing, that he had just slipped off into a deep dream. That wasn't the case of course. His eyes were closed and his face was slowly losing its red colour. He was still warm from the fever he had before. I sat there for a long time. Unaware of the world around me. The doctors however weren't unaware of what had just happened.

'Sir?' A soft voice spoke behind me.

'Yes?'

'Do you want me to take him...' further his sentence did not come. No further words were needed, I knew what he was talking about.

'Clear the burning spot, so there are no other ashes.' I took a deep breath. Trying to gather myself before continuing. The doctor had seemed to notice and waited patiently. 'I'll bring him there.'

'Of course.' The doctor said and moved away in silence. The rest of the doctors dared not to speak.

I looked at his hands, his gloves were still on. Now that his muscles weren't moving you could see the outline of the ring stand from the rest of his fingers. I took his glove off and took the ring as swiftly as I could; so no one would see me take it. I placed the cold ring on my own finger underneath my glove. They were the same type of gloves that Servius was wearing. He himself had given me the pair years back. The ones that I had used before were torn and old. Servius rarely bought gifts for people but he managed to give me some now and then. They were mainly books. Books about history, geography, or astronomy. Though once in a while he would give me a novel, always written in French. From a young age he had been pushing me to learn French and was more than happy to teach me himself. All Servius wanted me to do was learn. I don't carry any memories of Servius in which he isn't teaching me anything. I don't mind. Servius was the only teacher I ever had. Anything he would want to teach me I would gratefully learn.

My father's death had been a lesson for me. When he died Servius made me help carry him to the burning pile. I thought that that was the worst thing he would make me do, but I soon figured out that that had just been the beginning. He made me burn my own father. He made me start the fire. I did it. I always do what Servius asks me to do. I hated him for days. I truly believed that he was a monster, that he simply did it to hurt me. Only later I began to realize that this wasn't true. He made me the monster. He made me a monster that I never wanted to be. He wanted me to embrace something I was destined to be, but too scared to become.

CHAPTER 3

'Look at this closely Fransisco.' Servius said in a Low voice, looking at the blazing fire. Servius had to speak up to be heard over the loud crackling the fire made. He looked at the little boy standing next to him. He could see the fear in the boy's eyes.

'What's happening to them?' The small boy asked with a shaking voice.

'They meet their soul.' Servius said as the little boy shifted his weight between his legs. Servius stood in between him and the bridge, despite knowing the boy would never run away.

'Is that what a soul sounds like?' Fransisco moved his eyes to Servius. He admired Servius and his way of thinking. Servius knew this but neither of them ever spoke it out loud. It was an unspoken bond between them, both were scared to break.

'No.' Servius said simply, keeping his eyes fixed on Fransisco's.

'No?'

'We cannot hear souls. They're our greatest listeners.' He held Fransisco's gaze a little longer. Letting the words get to him before he continued. Fransisco knew how important it was to listen. Something Servius had drilled straight into his brain. "Listening is the greatest compliment you can give." He always used to say. Servius let go of his gaze, looking back to the blazing fire. 'We can fight them or live with them. We can learn to appreciate them or force them to change; for better or worse. But be careful, a soul is not something you can tame.'

'Will it destroy you?' Little Fransisco gasped.

'Not always.' Servius said after some careful consideration. 'Look at it like a tiger. If you seem like a threat to it, it will sneak up on you and attack. But if you treat it with respect and give it space you may be able to live alongside it. Give it time and you can become closer and closer to it, perhaps creating a friendship of sorts. But never rush. If you move too quickly or act too eager, it will become a threat, one of the worst kind. It will attack you with no means of stopping until you're dead. If you stand behind what you did, you will have to fight.'

The body that lay on the pile of wood had mostly burned away. The doctors hurried to the side, picking up another fresh corps to add to the fire.

'Have you found your soul?' Fransisco asked Servius. Thinking of the many scars Servius's body held, wondering if one of them had been made by his own soul.

'Don't go looking for it, you will find it before you're ready. Becoming a threat without even knowing it. Starting a fight you're not strong enough to win. Give it time, let it find you. It will never properly introduce itself to you with bad intentions.'

'If it never comes with bad intentions, why is it so dangerous?' Servius looked at the boy. The flames reflected in his eyes.

'The soul is a beautiful package with an unpleasant interieur.'

'Like the flames?'

'Like the flames, yes. Those who want the beautiful package will have to accept what comes within. And when the package becomes to leak there's nothing you can do about it.' The little boy stayed silent as the doctors put another body on the fire. A layer of ash was starting to form on the bottom. Now and then a gust of wind came, sweeping some of it away.

'So then why take the package?' He finally asked. Looking Servius in the eyes. Servius felt the boy loosening up. Forgetting all about the horrors that were taking place right in front of him. Nothing mattered more to him than what Servius was going to say next. Servius couldn't blame him. The boy thought to have found a way to create a path around all this trouble and pain. Servius knew at that moment that this wouldn't be the last time he was going to be the carrier of bad news.

'Because those who do not take it, will suffer all the more.'

CHAPTER 4

Servius was lying on the pile of wood. They had dragged him all the way from the infirmary to here; the burning grounds. His body lay still, waiting for the flames to come and take him. It had gotten late in the afternoon and almost every doctor and nurse had gathered around the pile of wood. They all looked at their feet, shuffling them a bit. I was waiting for someone to speak up but no one did. I took my gaze away from Servius and looked at the doctor standing to the left of me.

'Are you ready sir?' he asked uncertainly. His hand reached towards a stick in a small fire that stood beside him.

'Let me do it.' I said walking towards him.

'Are you sure that's a good idea, sir?' I didn't answer him. I wouldn't let him question me. My hands were shaking and sweat was building up on my forehead. This was mostly from the warmth of the sun that shone through the clear sky. I took the stick. My hand aching from the heat that managed to reach it. I turned it a bit, the flames dancing around. I carefully walked over to the pile of wood which held Servius. They had put his mask on his body, his hands resting on his stomach. I lowered the stick to the bottom of the pile. My eyes kept fixed on Servius. The moment the flames hit the wood it began to spread. I took away the stick and put it back in the small fire beside the doctor. I watched as the flames rose up quickly, soon reaching Servius. The smell of the burning leather hit me at once, making my eyes water. The flames had now risen enough that Servius was barely visible. The flames slowly took Servius away. Layer for layer. His clothing. His flesh. His muscle. All the way down to his bones. I stood there watching the whole process. Not noticing the time passing. Eyes drawn to the flames. The rest of the doctors stood with me. Not daring to walk away.

When his entire body was gone the flames settled down a little. His body was nothing more than a thin layer of ashes and the odd piece of bone that hadn't properly been burned yet. Bone was always hard to burn. Normally the fire would burn long enough, as multiple bodies were added to it, for the bones to completely turn into ash. But no bodies would be added now. So the bones were left. The flames left them as to say they had taken enough and were now full.

'Shall we collect it?' A doctor offered once all the flames were gone and the embers had lost their colours.

'Yes, you may. Put his ashes in this.' I said as I handed the doctor who was wearing thick gloves to protect him from the heat that was still left, a thick glass bottle. I knew it wasn't the most practical object to carry ashes in. I would hold the constant fear of the glass breaking. Spreading the ashes of my master as it did. Losing him forever. But that was just what I had wanted. Something fragile. Something that would force me to do my utter best to keep Servius safe. So I couldn't lose myself, because that could mean losing him.

With his ashes in my hand, I looked at what was left of the wooden pile. Secretly hoping Servius would appear from underneath it. Applauding me I had gotten through the test. That I was ready for the day that he would actually leave me. A day that would be far away from now.

I shook my head. Securing the glass bottle inside my robe. I tried my hardest to say something. To give a proper end to his leaving. But knew if I tried my voice would break. The doctors seemed to notice my troubles and gave me their sorrowful looks. Not one of them dared to say anything. I was thankful they didn't. As Servius was now gone it truly made me head of the island and that meant I couldn't be seen as weak. "As soon as you show weakness, trouble will come and find you." Servius used to tell me. Not daring to speak I simply nodded. The doctors didn't seem to be sure what this meant. I turned around. My head hung low as I made my way back to the infirmary.

I looked at the filled bottle in my hands. The ashes didn't add much weight and when I held it it almost felt like it wasn't there. Servius was gone. What was in this glass was the idea of Servius, the memories of Servius, but not he himself.

I never made it to the infirmary. Halfway through going there, I changed my route. Walking over to the waterline. Standing at the edge. Looking at the wide spread of water around me. Fiddling with the bottle in which lay Servius. The day had been nearing an end. The sun slowly beginning to set. I knew I had to get back to the infirmary. Servius would have hated to see me standing here. Drowning in thoughts that wouldn't help me. I placed the bottle back inside my cloak, keeping it close. There was work that had to be done, whether I was ready for it or not.

The hallways were filling themselves with doctors as I made my way through the front door of the infirmary. The sounds of doors creaking, shuffling footsteps and doctors talking grew like a cloak around me. The sounds were weary in the background as I got unsteady on my feet. My breathing quickened, filling my lungs with the filthy air that hung in the building. I tried to ignore it as I made my way through the hallway.

I stopped dead in my tracks as I heard them. Somewhere around me, I was sure I heard Servius talking to my father. I turned around and around, looking to see where the voices were coming from. Their talking began to sound more clearly as the rest of the sounds began fading away into the background. I shut my eyes, searching the direction of the sound. When I opened them they were right in front of me. My father sitting in a chair, Servius standing next to him. They were laughing, talking about me. I could see myself. A young little boy, sitting on the ground in front of them. I had made trouble, I knew. There was a big scar across my face. Servius was laughing. Proud that I had finally dared to make some trouble. My father on the other hand wasn't so happy. He was angry at me. Angry because I hadn't listened to him, and that was what had gotten me hurt. I had done something that would leave a scar on me. Something that I would never be able to get rid of.

I knew this wasn't really happening. But it felt so real. I wanted to talk to them. I wanted to hug my father one more time. Wanted to hear Servius his voice one more time as he spoke to me. Teaching me one more thing.

The room around me shifted. Everything became blurry at once. My feet only just managed to carry me through the door back outside. Breathing became difficult and panic started to rise. The world around me was swaying as I fell to my knees. Leaning my weight against a tree. Ripping my mask from my face. Wheezing as I tried to catch my breath. Feeling my heartbeat race as I put my hand on my chest. One of the doctors rushed towards me.

'Calm down, take a breath, you're going to be okay.' He said to me, kneeling down beside me. His voice sounded distant and I could just make out the words. I wanted to believe him but knew it wasn't true. Being okay wasn't something that would happen anytime soon. Things had changed today. Changed so much that it would never be able to go back to normal. Servius was truly gone now, nothing that this doctor could say would change that. He will never come back. I will never be able to speak to him again.

The whole world around me was black. All senses left my body. Only felt the cold air cut my skin, trying to escape each time I tried to breathe it in. My breathing began to calm down once a flowery drop of water hit my lips.

'This should help.' The same voice of the doctor said as he slowly moved away from me. Giving me some space. Air began to flow freely through my lungs. The world around me slowly reappeared as I sat down on the ground, leaning my back against the tree. My eyes were stuck on the grass near my feet. Slowly moving in the wind. There were birds tweeting around me as the setting sun shone on my face. The whole world had seemed to calm down.

Looking around me I saw a dozen eyes staring at me. Nothing I could do or say now would make up for what had just happened, so I decided to ignore them. Servius would have known what to do. Panic arose once again. I hurried to move my hand in my cloak. My heart skipped a beat as I did not feel it. Before I exploded in panic the doctor lay his hand on my shoulder, grabbing my attention. In his other hand, he tightly held the glass bottle. Knowing the value of what he was holding he quickly handed it back over to me. I held it with both hands as I gave a great full nod to the doctor. He gave me a weak smile in return. The doctors that had gathered around slowly drifted away. Each one of them back to their dull lives. Only the doctor still kneeled beside me didn't move. Nor did he speak. He simply waited as I held the bottle close to me. Getting myself back together before I could continue on. I gave him a little nod.

'You can go.' I said

'Are you sure?' he asked. It shouldn't have angered me but something about his tone made me feel small.

'Yes, I'm sure!' I said rather loud. The doctor jumped up and hurried away. The heels of my shoes made a little carving in the damp grass. Doctors and nurses were making their way in and out of the infirmary. All their eyes scanned me as they walked past. I knew that I would look back on this and feel shame. But knowing that didn't mean I did something about it. My mind seemed lost. Busy pondering over the friend I lost. Knowing inside that it was better to let him go, but stuck in reliving the good times. The times that Poveglia seemed a little brighter.

Letting go of it would be good. With him the good times should go, so the bad times could too. The times I'd rather not think of anymore but kept creeping in from time to time. Servius had suffered for a long time. My ignorance keeping him with me. Servius had finally stopped suffering, which meant that my suffering had just begun. Whatever I would do that was a burden I was now carrying. A burden that by no means would leave anytime soon. If Servius saw me like this he would grab me and pull me up at once. He would be right in my face. "Something wrong with your legs? If your legs can't keep you up you shouldn't be here. Poveglia isn't a place for rest." His stern voice would tell me. So I stood up, brushed off the dirt on my knees, and put back on my mask. Looking straight ahead as I walked away from the main hospital, back to the housing of the island.

CHAPTER 5

The little path that led to the front door of Servius's house was overgrown with plants. They were sprouting out from underneath rocks, between the tiles of the path, and even seemed to grow out of the bricks of the house. They weren't nice plants, with pretty flowers growing out of them. They were all bare ugly ones, that grow even though there's no sunlight. Those about whom you question if it is even possible for them to die.

Servius had never given much care to the plants around his house. Not that he had enough time if he wanted to. But things had slowly become worse. It somewhat hurt me to see that Poveglia was being abandoned. It had started slowly but the change quickly grew as the urgency of Poveglia wore off. It had been two years since Servius had died and the Poveglia now is nothing like it had been then. There had been fewer sick people coming onto Poveglia, but as always none had left the island alive. I'm certain that even the dead never get to leave Poveglia behind. Their souls stuck on the island desperately trying to get away. With the amount of people who died on Poveglia, I hope that souls can walk through each other.

Servius was with them now. Bound to the island. I am sure I'm going to end up here too. I have already given up the last bit of hope I had of being able to escape. There was no use. Even if Poveglia would become empty I wouldn't be able to leave. My soul was stuck here, alongside Servius. I would leave it behind the moment I stepped off the island.

I think I have accepted it by now. It almost seemed like something to look forward to. To leave my body behind and only exist in the form of a soul. Being reunited with Servius. And my father. I had forgotten about my father. Forgotten the reason I was bound to this island in the first place. Maybe that's why I had forgotten him. Forgotten because the consequences of his actions were greater than the memories I ever made with him.

But I couldn't blame him. Not for putting me here. It wasn't all nice growing up here, but it might have been better than it would have been if he hadn't taken me here. I can hardly remember anything from the first four years of my life. My father had never really wanted to talk about it. For years I had thought that I was born here, on the island.

Until Servius accidentally let something slip about the past I never knew I had.

The paint had mostly been peeled off the front door. Leaving an ugly washed-out colour behind. The door was slightly bent on the bottom, which would have made for a draft during the winter. I was struggling as I kept twisting the key and was about to give up when the door finally let go of its strength and opened up. The door gave a loud creak as I pushed it open. I stood on the doorstep, looking inside. Dust was dancing through the air. I took a deep breath. The smell the house had, which Servius had given it, was untraceable.

I was nervous to enter his house. In these two years before I had entered the house once and again, but only now was I cautious. This would be one of the last times that I would be able to come here. To look at his stuff for one last time. Deciding what I would take, what would be thrown away, and what would be left here to rot.

His house was simplistic. There weren't many things besides the necessary items. There was a small kitchen, though Servius rarely cooked. A big bookcase takes over an entire wall and a wooden table with three chairs stands in the middle of the room. There was plenty more space that could be filled but Servius had never seen reasons to.

The only times all three chairs at the table were filled was when me and my father were here. We would now and then get together to eat dinner. It was always my father who insisted it would be fun. Servius would grunt a bit about it but would always give in.

I walked up the stairs, each one creaked as I put my weight on it. I stopped on the last stair. Looking up at a painting that hung on the wall. There was only one painting in his house, Servius wasn't that interested in them. But this one he hung up. I remember making it. It was a painting of Servius and me standing near the edge of the island. Wearing our doctors' clothes, and masks on our heads. Behind us towered the hospital building with on the end the bell tower that was looming over us. He never told me he had hung it up, so months after when I saw it hanging here I couldn't be more proud. Servius never used to care about giving and receiving presents. But with me, he always tried.

I think I made him that way. My father used to tell me that and after some time I started to believe it. I started to pay more attention to what Servius did and my father had been right. But being so absorbed by what Servius did, maybe I chose only what I wanted to believe.

I can't remember how Servius was when I was little. According to my father, he didn't care for me. But when I grew up we became closer. After my father had died especially. He had begun to see me as his own son.

There are three rooms upstairs. A small bathroom, a small bedroom, and a workroom. The houses on Poveglia weren't big. But because of that many houses could fit, and all the doctors and nurses were able to sleep on the island. Servius had the largest one on the island and still, it was only just big enough to live in.

I walked through the tiny hallway into the workroom. That's what Servius used to call it. There was a small wooden desk with a chair neatly tucked underneath it. Another bookshelf took over the wall and in the corner near a window, there stood another table. This one however was round and short, but very thick.

Carved on the wooden table were nine circles. Each of the holes in the table was the same size. The holes lay in the way of small circles that were carved around the whole table. There lay a little bag on the table. Curious that I hadn't seen it before I picked it up. The little bag was made of leather and was knotted close by a little robe on the top. I carefully opened the bag and inside there were eight wooden balls. I spread them out over the table. Each ball had been painted in different colours. I quickly understood what I had to do. I grabbed the green and blue ball and placed it in the third ring. After that, I took the orange one and put it in the second ring. Then the blue, the red, the light blue, the grey and the yellow one. So at last I was holding one more. One that had been painted with white, yellow, orange, and browns. I had always thought Jupiter was the most beautiful planet of them all. I carefully placed it in the only spot that was left open.

There was a soft click. In shock, I took a step back and watched what happened. The wood had shifted, but only slightly. There was a tiny bit of space between the wood that was sticking out and the table itself. My hand reached forward. As I put my fingers on the table I wondered if was a good idea to open it. After all, I didn't know what was hidden inside. What I would be letting loose. But Servius had made it, right? If it was a part of him then perhaps I did know what was inside.

The wood of the little drawer that had clicked out was cracked and a slightly different colour than the rest of the table. I wedged my fingers between the drawer and the table and gave a little tug. Bit by bit the drawer began to give way. The drawer wouldn't open very far, but just enough for my hand to squeeze in and take what was hidden inside. In the drawer was a wooden gourd. Carved from dark wood embraced with details. It was rather large and round on the bottom half, which was shaped into an hourglass, only to come out as a smaller version of the bottom on the top. I turned this around in my hands, wondering what the function was of this rather odd object to keep hidden. It couldn't simply have been decoration.

A text had been carved in the bottom of it. "Terminee aujourd'hui 18 de 7embre 1793 jean roux citoyen Parisian auteur" it hadn't surprised me that the text had been written in French. Servius had always had an interest in France. Besides him speaking the language he would often flip through the newspaper looking for news about France. I wouldn't know if it was simply out of interest that he searched for news of France or that there was more to it. I never asked about it but observed him quite a bit when he was reading. Often shaking his head as if in disbelief. Once I thought I had heard him mutter "I should never have left." under his breath. But I could have easily been wrong.

There were many other things written all over the gourd, but most of it was faded away and difficult to read. The only thing I could discover was a name. Maximilien Robespierre. A French name, no question about it. But I didn't recognise it. I had never heard of it nor read it in any paper. I assumed he was the person who had made the gourd. A worker of detail, a writer at soul. But why had he made this?

I kept turning the wooden gourd around until it felt like I could redraw all the details from memories. I saw a vague line that traced the whole middle part of the gourd. I tried to turn the sides away from each other. Carefully putting strength in it as the gourd opened up. My hands were shaking barely holding on to the gourd. I twisted the opening towards me so I could peer into the darkness inside. However, that darkness had a rather dark red colour. My hand reached towards something I thought was a red handkerchief but ended up being a handkerchief covered in blood.

My shaking hands took the handkerchief out of the gourd. The blood that had soaked it had hardened over time. I tugged at it, but it didn't move. It had completely molded itself to the shape of the gourd. The handkerchief wasn't much bigger than my hand. But the blood made it a lot more bulky. I wondered what the reason was that Servius had kept this. It was something that wasn't ordinary for Servius to have. It almost made me think Servius might have not known it was here, but that would probably be unlikely. Many questions began popping up in my brain.

Unsure of what it all meant I put the handkerchief back in the gourd and closed it back up. Just as I had done that I heard footsteps running up the stairs. I quickly hid the gourd in my cloak. Keeping it near Servius, whom in these two years, I had always carried with me. For a moment I thought I was losing it again but realised I had left the front door open. Daring to enter Servius's house took a nerve that most doctors did not have. So who was walking up the stairs?

'Fransisco?' a small voice came from outside the door. A woman's voice, one I immediately recognised.

'Alice!' of course it had been her. She was the only one on the island besides myself who dared to enter Servius's house. After Servius's death, she had been keeping a close eye on me. Together we walked to our house after the long days of work and in the morning we walked back to the hospital. It had been nice to have her company. She could never replace Servius of course. Her main goal after his death had been to keep me from going insane. I wouldn't say it had been successful, as processing the loss of Servius wasn't something I was any good at. Getting stuck in a loop of grief day after day.

'Are you okay? You haven't been here in a while.' she said. Of course, she knew. The only thing that annoyed me about her was that she made it almost impossible to be alone. I couldn't escape from the world's eyesight. Not anymore.

'I suppose you've heard the news.' I said changing the subject as fast as I could.

'Yes, of course. Everyone is talking about it! Barely any sick people, that's wonderful isn't it?' She took a dubious step into the room. Looking around her, eyes wide, amazed by what Servius had placed in his house. I had never let her enter. Wanting to keep this place for me alone. For me and Servius.

'Wonderfull, as you said, yes.' her eyes shot to me.

'You don't seem convinced of it? You don't think it's wonderful?' She asked. Tilting her head a little to the right.

'I don't know. It feels rather… I don't know; narrowing, perhaps.'

'Narrowing?' I saw the disbelieve in her eyes, knowing she didn't get what I meant. I wasn't even sure that I got it.

'Yes, fewer people getting sick, which is great. But the ones that are still here are doomed to die. You know it. Has anyone ever left Poveglia alive? No. The stream of sick people is only narrowing.'

'But soon it will stop. Then we can all go, live a normal life.' I grunted as she spoke those words.

'I don't think any of us will have a normal life after this.'

'Won't we?'

'Will we?' She looked at me. This comment had Cleary annoyed her. I knew why. She hadn't found a cure. Alice had spent her years on Poveglia searching for a cure, and after all this time there was still nothing that worked. I knew it bothered her greatly. She liked to believe that that would all be forgotten the moment she left the island but I knew that this was something she would carry with her for the rest of her life. They all had to, no one would forget about what had happened on Poveglia.

'All I'm saying is that you should have a little hope.'

'And all I'm saying is that you shouldn't ignore the reality, and face the troubles that may arise. To let go of that hope a little.'

'Why? Why let go of something so beautiful?'

'Because it isn't true.' she sat down on the chair placed behind the desk. I didn't like her being in the house. Making use of what had once been Servius's.

'Do you dream?'

'What?' I said, rather annoyed.

'When you fall asleep, do you see him?' her eyes were locked on mine.

'Servius?' She gave a little nod. I looked through the door into the hallway. There was some light shining through a little window. I imagined him standing there. Putting on his mask. Getting ready for a day rotten with death.

'I don't have to fall asleep for that. I see him everywhere I go.' she didn't answer right away. I could see her try to hide the disgust she felt for this. It wasn't normal for me to see Servius, which I knew, but it didn't bother me. It was a great comfort to me that I saw Servius. Servius never spoke to me and neither did I to him. I couldn't see why it could hurt me to have his company.

'What you could try is-,'

'I don't want to change it. I like his company.'

'People will think you're crazy.' She said in protest.

'Am I not?'

31

CHAPTER 6

Poveglia shut down soon after that.

Many of the doctors were packing up their things. Only a few would stay longer on the island, as there were still a few people in the hospital who needed to die. It was their responsibility to make sure no traces were left. That these people could die in peace and follow the road many others had walked before them. Getting their bodies burned and their ashes thrown away with the rest. Stories would be the only thing that told what had happened on the island.

I was one of the ones who was bound to the island for a little longer. It had been up to me to choose who would leave now and who would stay. Alice was the first on my list. She believed she could live a normal life once leaving the island behind. So holding her back wasn't an option for me.

Who else would be able to leave wasn't so easy to decide. There were many good doctors on Poveglia, all the bad ones had either gotten sick or left. After some pondering the decision was made. I would keep two nurses and five doctors on the island. That would be enough to take care of the work that was left. There were about 30 people left in the hospital, no more were entering. It was only a matter of time before the last ones would die. Then our work started. Burning all the bodies, getting rid of their ashes. A process that took longer with fewer hands. Not that mine helped. I wanted nothing to do with the last deaths on the island.

I kept busy with all the paperwork. Making sure that every name was on a list. Making sure there was nothing left to do when the time came to leave this place behind. That everything was written down in such a way that I wasn't to worry about it anymore. With all the papers flying around me I knew there was no way I would ever forget what happened here. The only other chair in the room had stacks of paper on it. The stack wasn't at all straight and was dangerously close to falling off.

I couldn't get around the last death of Poveglia. There was no going back. I had to look beyond the paperwork and into the infirmary. The dim lighting was more gloomy than ever as I walked through the empty hallway. The creaking floor seemed louder than before, exaggerated by the silence around it. For a moment it felt like everyone had already left the island except me. Only the distant voices of the doctors talking gave away that this wasn't the truth.

The big door to the infirmary was open and the moment I stepped in the doctors stopped talking. All eyes turned towards me in shock. They apparently hadn't heard my footsteps approaching. They all stood in a circle around a hospital bed that was placed at the end of the room. I was the last one to attend.

As I got closer the doctors took a step back. Creating a space for me to enter their circle. I stepped amidst them, looking at the corpse that lay in the hospital bed. The last one to die.

'This is her, sir.' On the bed lay an old woman, dressed in a hospital gown, neatly tugged away underneath a blanket. Her hair was grey and her face was full of wrinkles. She was way beyond her young years, but she has a face I remember; and a name I wouldn't dare to speak. She had been here for a long while now. She had two grandchildren whom she loved to talk about. They were both boys at about the age of seven. They loved it when she cooked for them.

From the moment she got here, she knew how it would end for her. She has kept telling her stories to anyone who would listen. Desperate to have something life on when she wouldn't be around anymore. Something that would never be forgotten. We will never forget her. She had made many friends in the hospital. Other patients as well as the doctors and nurses.

We had always known she would be the last to die. She had been the strongest of all. For a while, I had hoped that she would survive. That she would get better and would be able to go back to her family. But hope is not always enough.

It saddened me to look at her dim eyes, her gaze fixed on something that was beyond this world. I walked towards her and took off my gloves. Something I had only dared to do once before. It felt right to do when Servius was dying and it felt right now. They weren't just patients to me, they were people who had suffered. My hand stretched out towards the motionless body. I gently placed my fingertips on her eyelids. They were still warm. I thought of Servius as I pulled down the eyelids so they were closed. Making it look like she was sleeping rather than dead. I took my hand back quickly and put my glove back on.

'It's a shame she had to be last.' one of the doctors started. 'She was wonderful, had amazing stories. She didn't deserve to die here on this gloomy island.'. The doctors and nurses around him nodded. Each one of them was looking at the ground.

'At least we were here for her.' a nurse added. At this, the doctors around her all muttered yes. All proud of the company they had given her when she had been the only one left. She had been for weeks. Even though they were confident the attention they had given her was good; I thought differently. We weren't the company she deserved. I had only talked to her once when Servius had died. I was ashamed to admit I never much thought about her after that. And I knew this was true for many other doctors as well. I knew it hadn't been nice for her. She should have been surrounded by her friends and family. Ones that didn't keep count of how long it took for her to die. We weren't that. I surely hadn't been. She had never even seen my face.

My plague mask kept everything I felt and thought neatly hidden. Feelings had to be hidden at times. "Crying isn't for leaders." Servius told me whenever he saw tears building up in my eyes. I had never dared to cry, scared that people would label me as weak. Never until Servius died. Tears had been streaming down my face when I spoke to him. Seeing him laying in the hospital bed, so close to dying. When he took his last breath. While I watched his body burn; when his ashes were put in a bottle. None of the doctors knew this. The mask had kept it well hidden. The mask couldn't keep it hidden from Servius. I'm sure he had known. He often gave me a soft look. As if he knew I was crying. But he never said anything about it.

'Let's move her.' I said. My voice was harsh, more so than I meant. I took a step back, making room for the nurses. Speaking anymore would probably end with tears filling my eyes and a cracking voice, so I kept silent. Watching the nurses preparing the old woman to be taken away. They worked quickly as they put her on the transport bed. The doctors each took hold of her and together they carried her to the burning pile.

Once she was on it the fire was started. Some of the doctors walked away, it would take a while before she was gone and now that everyone had died a lot of work was to be done before they could leave the island for good. This was the last time I would see someone get burned. The last soul that would be bound to the island and so I decided to stay.

Once she had been burned and everything had been cooled down they collected all the ashes, putting them in a large pot. None of the doctors knew what to say and so together we all walked towards the empty sea. The blue waves hitting the side of the island were small. The sky was blue and the sun shone bright in our faces. We each took a handful of ash from the big pot. I took last and took what was left in the pot. I took a step closer to the edge. I took a deep breath and swung my arm, opening my hand at the right time so the ashes flew out over the water. Dancing around in the air a bit before they were mixed with the sea. The rest followed my lead.

It didn't take long before the entirety of Poveglia was shut down. All the paperwork was put into boxes and placed on the little boats that were sailing from and towards Venice. It didn't take long before they were back at the little port of Poveglia. Ready to be filled once more. This cycle went on for the rest of the day. Slowly emptying the island.

I was running around for most of the day. Trying to get everything ready to be loaded on, making sure everyone was helping out. This wasn't something that I liked doing, but I also didn't mind it enough to give this job to anyone else. Set aside that I would trust anyone to do it.

'Is this all the paperwork?' the nurse beside me asked. I was looking over the little port. There were three boats bound to the island. Doctors were filling them with boxes. Further off in the distance, you could see two more little boats making their way to the island. The water was a little rough and the sky was filled with clouds. I held my mask in my arms, not needing to wear it anymore but feeling rather naked without it.

'There is still a little more in my office, but that's being taken care of.' I said. the nurse beside me whistled. 'Yeah, it's a lot. A lot of people have died here.'

'Do the families know they're dead?'

'Yes, I'm sure they do.'

'Yeah?' she said. I looked towards her, our eyes met for a moment. Her eyes had a twinkle, a spark of hope. Mine didn't. I knew that. She noticed too, as the sparkle in her eyes slowly disappeared.

'They know that Poveglia is shut down. It's in almost every paper. Their loved ones won't come back. That is enough for them to know that they're dead. Isn't it?'

'I supposed.' the nurse said gloomily. 'I just hoped it would be different, you know?' I waited for her to continue. She took a deep breath before she did. It sounded like the was searching for the only bit of fresh air that could be found on Poveglia. A breath that wouldn't be filled with death. 'They shouldn't have to wait in agony. They should have known the moment they passed away.'.

'That would be impossible. There have been too many deaths here. It would take more than 50 people to tell everyone when someone has died. What if they did it? Would their waiting be any different?' she waited a moment before she spoke. Her eyes were fixed on the ground. There was a small of me that felt bad for what I had said.

'You knew when Servius died.' she waited. I felt her regret the moment she had finished her sentence. She didn't do anything to make it right, to change what she had just said. Maybe I had asked for such an answer. That didn't mean I liked hearing it.

'Servius and I, that was different. I wouldn't have known Servius if I had never been on this island. I wouldn't have waited in agony.'

'Would you have preferred it?' she hesitantly asked.

'Preferred what?'

'Not knowing Servius, not needing to go through it; his death.' I had never pondered about this question before. I had never thought of the possibility of not having known Servius.

'No. I'm happy I've known him. Seeing him die wasn't nice, but I got an ending. If he would still be alive now... After Poveglia, who knew what would have happened? Maybe Servius would have left me. Walked off on his own, never to speak to me again. I would have constantly been worrying about him.' she nodded but didn't look at me.

'I would have rather not known my husband than see him die.'.

'Good thing Servius isn't my husband.' she laughed at that. I laughed too, but didn't feel like it.

'Do you miss him?'

'Yes.' she looked me in the eyes. The smile had vanished as quickly as it had appeared.

'You look gloomy.' she said, as she changed her position so that she was now standing in front of me. My eyes couldn't find anything other than her to look at. 'Eyes can tell a lot about someone. They can hide how they feel in their smile but their eyes can't hide secrets. I haven't often seen your eyes, you've been hiding them well under that mask.'

'That's what It's for isn't it, hiding?'

'I suppose.'. There was a little pause. 'You plague doctors don't seem to have any emotions when I look at that mask. And your voices are all the same as well. I won't lie, once you grew up and, were about

Servius's height, I often couldn't tell which of you was who. I have called your master Fransisco many times; you know. Each time he would laugh at me for getting it wrong. "Yes that boy is growing up" he used to say. He was proud of you. You were the most important thing to him.'

'That time is over now.'

'I don't think so. I don't think he ever stopped being proud of you. Not even now. His body might be lost, but his soul is still here.' she said pointing at my chest. I gave her an uncertain look.

'His soul is not with me. His feelings don't matter anymore. His feelings, his thoughts, are lost.'

'But that doesn't mean that they don't exist anymore.' she was a thinker; optimistic. She didn't care what happened, she only took the positive part of it. Something I was glad I didn't do.

'We should get going.' she looked at me like she had won. That it could only be right to look at the good parts. I didn't say anything about it and walked away in a hurry.

I picked up the last box that was left on the island and brought it over to the boats. The box was small and light. I dropped the box in the boat and walked away from it, signing to one of the doctors to go first. He stepped in the little boat, making it sway as soon as he put his weight on it.

The doctors stepped, one after another, into the little boats. Being sailed away from the island.

'I hope to see you once more, Fransisco.' the nurse said as she stepped into the boat. I gave her a little nod, knowing that I was never to see her again. My job wasn't done yet, I had one more task I had to complete.

As her little boat sailed off I was the last on the island. I wasn't truly alone, the sailer of the little boat looked around him nervously. His eyes moved along the side of the island like he was waiting for a corpse to come around the corner to snatch him from his boat. Dragging him into the water, never to be seen again. I didn't want to make him wait any longer. I looked behind me quickly. Taking in the buildings. This would be the last time I would stand on this island. Leaving behind everything I had known. I felt the ring on my finger, the little glass bottle in my cloak, and checked once more if the gourd was in my suitcase. With everything in order I couldn't think of another reason I could delay my goodbye.

I shuffled my way over to the boat, placing my suitcase in it. I turned around another time to look at the island. It had never been this silent before. There were no people outside, the only thing that could be heard was the wind moving through the trees, and the waves hitting the side of the island. I would leave this place behind. I would never come back. This was it, the end. Now that the time was here, that I could finally leave, I wasn't so sure that I wanted to. I would be leaving more behind than I originally thought I would. Leaving a part of me behind. Almost all of me. This had been my past and present. Leaving behind my father. But most importantly leaving behind Servius. He was bound to stay here, I was leaving behind a part of Servius that would never return. The only memories left of him locked in the glasses of my mask.

He stood in front of me. Appearing from around the corner, standing there, looking at me. His mask on his face, his hands hidden inside the pockets of his cloak. He looked at me and knew that I was looking at him. He didn't speak, didn't walk towards me. He just stood there, watching as I would leave. I had to. I had to turn around and step into the little boat that would bring me to Venice. I gave Servius a little nod, which he reflected. And so I left. The boat felt unstable under my feet as I got in. A feeling that lessened with every meter we sailed away from Poveglia.

I watched Servius get smaller. Still standing in the same spot, waiving me goodbye.

CHAPTER 7

It made a great splash when Francisco jumped in the water. It had been a long warm day in the midst of the summer. There hadn't been a cloud to give Poveglia a little shade. Once Servius and Fransisco finished the day's work their uniform had been soaked in sweat.

Fransisco didn't need to think twice when Servius suggested they go swimming. Fransisco was the first to jump in the water but it didn't take long before Servius followed his lead. Fransisco floated on his back, squinting his eyes. He heard the doctors who stood at the edge of the water muttering. It wasn't usual to go swimming in the waters of Poveglia. The other doctors were scared of what lay in the water. Servius wasn't. Fransisco had asked him about it earlier in the summer when Servius first brought this idea into his mind.

Fransisco had of course fantasised about jumping in many times before, but his father never let him. He was clearly scared of what was hidden beneath the peaceful waves that hit the side of the island. Servius had called it "utter bullshit". He believed that if the simple idea was enough for the doctors to be scared away from something they could never be great doctors. And so one warm day, when his father wasn't around, Servius had taken Fransisco to go swim. His father had been furious when he found out what he did. Servius had sent Fransisco away before he spoke to his father. He never knew what he said but it had seemed to work. His father never spoke of it again.

'Refreshing ain't it?' Servius said loudly. Fransisco opened his eyes and looked over at Servius, who was swimming around aimlessly. Behind Servius, Fransisco could see the doctors. They had been staring at them but, at Servius's words, they quickly looked away and pretended to get back to work. Servius knew what his words had done and quickly winked at Fransisco. Fransisco chuckled.

The water was starting to cool his body off as he swam towards Servius. Servius noticed and waited for Fransisco to catch up to him. Slightly out of breath Fransisco reached Servius and got close to him.

'What if we quietly swim up to them, and then grab their feet and drag them in?' Fransisco whispered. A large grin began forming on Servius's face.

'I think that's a great idea kid.' Servius said as a took a quick glance at the edge. 'I'll distract them by swimming by, you drag them in.' He said. Servius had swum off before Fransisco could agree. The doctors brought back their gaze to Servius as he swam by. Fransisco swiftly started moving towards the edge.

Careful to make as little noise as possible.

Once at the edge, he looked up to see if he had been spotted. But all the doctors were way too busy with Servius swimming to have noticed him coming near. He chose his victim and moved himself along the edge so that he was right underneath him. He looked over his shoulder, to see if Servius was paying attention. Servius met his gaze and gave a quick nod.

Fransisco pushed himself up the edge and with his right hand grabbed the leg of the doctor that stood in front of him. The doctor let out a loud high-pitched scream and jumped back. Fransisco wasn't fast or strong enough to pull him into the water. But the scared reaction of all the doctors, in addition to the scream itself, had Fransisco and Servius roaring with laughter. Servius had moved himself to the edge, placing a hand on Fransisco's shoulder.

'Well done kid.' He said. At that moment, Fransisco felt very proud.

CHAPTER 8

Venice wasn't what I had imagined it to be. I had never been to Venice before but had put together an image from the stories Servius had told me. Empty barren streets and unfriendly people. But what stood in front of me was quite the contrary. There were boats everywhere. Almost filling up the entire sea. Big ships filled with goods. With loads of people running around on them, unloading what was hidden inside. But there weren't only big ships. Small boats navigated their way around the bigger ships, in the water that seemed to stream through the whole city. The streets were stuffed with people buzzing about. It was like the plague had never existed here.

Servius had often gone to Venice. I was never allowed to go with him. He told me this was a dangerous place. There would be no people outside, all hiding from the thing they feared most. Hidden inside their houses scared to get in contact with anyone outside their family. Each staying in their own little bubble. Their own fantastical world in which they were safe. The sound of the wind would be overpowering and the waters would be dirty. Animals would roam the streets, wondering where everyone had gone.

I had never doubted the descriptions Servius had given me. Although they never stopped me from wanting to join Servius away from the island. To see this so said disaster, happy when the time came to go back to Poveglia.

I wandered through the narrow streets, without a plan of where to go. It was still early on in the day so there was no hurry to find a place to stay. Besides, all the people knew me here. Their gazes followed me, making way for me as I approached them in the streets. They knew me as the demon from hell who had come here to make them all sick and get them all killed. I couldn't stay here, no one would want me.

And so I continued walking through the streets, getting closer and closer to the heart of the city. At least, that's what I thought I was doing. It quickly became clear that things weren't exactly going as planned. I got a little lost, with no way to go but forward.

After walking for a little I got to the part of the city where the streets couldn't be any narrower. I looked around me, the buildings hiding any sign of where I was to go. Behind me, the street was filling up with people. Staying close together so as not to get too close to me. There was no other option for me but to go forward.

It was a small bridge crossing a part of the sea that roamed through the city. It was barricaded by buildings all around it, which were taken over by flowers, growing on its sides. Everything seemed to be one big construction rather than smaller individual houses. There was a group of children walking towards me. They were wearing old clothes and had the amount of energy contained, I didn't know one could hold without exploding. They were running around one another, screaming and laughing.

I moved to the right side of the bridge, preparing myself for the tornado of laughter that would pass me. Grasping onto the mask, which I was still holding in my hand, scared that one of the kids would try to take it away from me. But what they did was rather unexpected. They stopped dead in their tracks, looking at me. I was bracing myself for the burst of laughter, the hurtful words when they told me I didn't belong here. But that didn't happen. They gave me a careful smile and continued on. One stayed behind for a second longer, interestedly looking at the mask I was holding. I held the mask a little tighter, holding it close to my body. Not really sure if I was trying to hide it or trying to protect it. There had been no use hiding it, as the boy had already seen what it was. But he didn't know the value it held. The memories and feelings it had captured over the years. The mystery that lay within. But he left, running after the other boys who were already some streets away. Still chasing each other, while screaming and laughing.

They hadn't been scared of me. They hadn't stared at me with a weird look in their eyes. Putting great effort into walking around me, staying as far away from me as possible. They acted like I was a normal person. Someone who wasn't linked to pain and dying. That what I was wearing and carrying in my arms was normal. A sight everyone saw every day.

I didn't know what else to do but continue. I unclenched my fists a bit, loosening the grip around the mask but still holding it close. I had been so scared, scared of what would happen to me when in the end, all that happened was nothing.

Soon I found my way into the actual heart of the city. There were fewer people than I expected. Which may have been because the streets were a lot wider here. The building which stood at the side of these streets rose even higher than the ones I had seen before.

After I while I stopped walking. I looked up at the building that stood at my feet. It was a big stone building filled with windows and light. These lights were shining bright against the sky. Which hadn't turned dark yet. The big doors to the building were open. It couldn't have been more inviting. But I knew I wasn't to go in. People wouldn't want a plague doctor in such a beautiful building. They would fix their gaze on me and never let me go.

They would fear me, they always had. Now that the plague was "gone" that wouldn't change. I was still like a demon to them. A demon that would ruin their life once they got too close. A darkness that would overtake them when they least expect it. Their fear of me was still here, something they would be unable to get rid of.

Even though I knew that I could not go inside I decided it couldn't hurt to get a closer look at it. I walked up the little stairs that led to the main doors. There were multiple newspapers placed in front of the door together with some sort of flyer. I picked one up, struggling to hold it in the same hand that was holding my mask. I opened the flyer, looking at the text written inside. The flyer was red, with a picture of a large building painted on it. I didn't recognise the building, but it looked even bigger than the one in front of me. The writing on the inside was small and difficult to read but I understood what was there.

It was some sort of big pawn shop, selling only the most beautiful pieces of art. Art from France. Rome was taken over by the French, up until now that had been the only news I had ever heard about Rome. The gallery was free for everyone to enter, getting them accustomed to the French culture.

I looked at the suitcase I was holding. The writing on the gourd had been French. I had never heard of the person who made the gourd, but it could have been a French artist. I didn't know who Servius's wife was and I was certainly never going to find out if I stayed here in Venice. So Rome it would be.

I decided I would go look for a horse. With that, I would be able to ride all the way to Rome. I would find a place to stay there and then I would go the the pawn shop. It would be open for another while so there wasn't much hurry.

I started to notice that people around me were fixing their gaze on me. The workers inside were talking to one another in a low voice, pointing fingers at me. Quickly acting like they weren't talking about me when I looked over at them. I turned around, hoping I would get away from there without anyone talking to me. And most importantly without any authorities going after me.

Servius had told me that had happened to him once. He was walking through the streets holding his plague mask under his arm. Some guy thought he was dangerous and made it his job to get rid of this danger. He took Servius and dragged him all through Venice to the police. The police had let him go without much trouble. Not because he hadn't done anything wrong, but because they didn't want him there. They didn't want to lock him up in case he would get sick. It would have been too much of a risk for them to get sick. They were scared of him and that's why they let him go. Cowards.

That's not what I should be focusing on now. I should try and get myself to Rome as fast as I could. There I would decide what to do next. There I will find out who Maximilien is, and why Servius has something from him.

I wouldn't know where other to start. When Servius was dying all I was thinking about was how I was going to lose him. That he would go away and never return. That I would still be here, without him. I can't do this without him. I had never been in the open world, had never left Poveglia. I didn't know how things worked. Servius knew. Servius knew everything. I knew nothing.

I had to get to Rome, I kept reminding myself as my thoughts wandered off. It was the only place I could think of to start and I better option I did not have. The only way of getting there was by horse, it was simply too far away to walk. Only a small problem, I had never ridden a horse in my life before. Thought it didn't seem all that difficult to me. There were loads of people around this part of Venice who rode a horse. So there was no reason for me to believe I couldn't too.

'Miss, excuse me.' I said to a lady who was walking towards me in the streets. She quickly took a step back, fear gleaming in her eyes. Before I could say anything else she had run away from me. She looked over her shoulder every few meters or so to make sure that I wasn't following her. Which I didn't.

'That's not a nice way to treat a young man like you.' an old lady said. She stood to the right of me, arm in arm with an old man, that seemed to be her husband. They were both rather small but didn't seem that frightened by me.

'I don't think I'm that kind.' I said, giving a small smile to the lady.

'Anyone who starts their sentence with "excuse me" seems like a kind person. Now what's the matter? You seem rather lost, maybe we can help you.' She said as she pushed her elbow into the side of the man standing next to her. He shot up, like he had awoken from his dream, and nodded his head with enthusiasm. The old lady smiled at him, happy with the reaction he had given.

'I am looking for a stable where I could buy a horse.' The old lady smiled as she made herself a little taller.

'That is nearby here! Just follow this road and soon you'll be able to leave the city. The stable is straight in front of you there, you won't be able to miss it.' She said beaming. Happy that she knew the answer, that she could help me.

'Thank you.' I said as I gave a little nod. I could see that she was delighted that I thanked her. Her smile was so wide I couldn't help myself smiling back at her.

I waved at them as I followed the lady's instructions to keep walking. It didn't take me long before I got outside of the city. Where the stable soon got in my view. It was small and hiding behind trees that had taken over the places of the houses. It was made of wooden planks and stones. The closer I got the smaller the stable was than I had expected.

There was hay lying around everywhere you looked. The ground was completely covered with it and it was hanging on the walls. If I didn't know better I would say they only kept hay here, and not actual horses. I had never been in a stable before, but Servius had told me much about them. He wasn't so fond of them. He called them gross and smelly, but necessary.

I made my way into the hay-covered stables. There were people inside busy sweeping the floor. Something that clearly didn't seem to do anything.

'Hello sir, how may I help you? I turned around, surprised by the sudden greeting I had gotten. The man who stood in front of me was dressed in a brown pair of pants and a light blue blouse. His hair was red and stood bewildered on his head. His face was covered with dirt and in his hands he held onto something that had once been a broom.

'I would like to buy a horse.' I said. The man laughed. He looked at me, taking me in, with a look that told me all I needed to know.

'A horse? For you?' My hand tightened around the mask.

'Yes please, one that is able to take me all the way to Rome.' the man looked at me and leaned against his broom. He noticed that I wasn't joking.

'What has a man like you to do in Rome? Shouldn't you be gone, kept far away from people?' Anger started to rise in me.

'What I have to do in Rome is none of your business. Do you have a horse for me or not?' He shifted his weight between his legs. He clearly wasn't happy with what I had said to him. When it became clear to him that I wouldn't simply walk away he decided to help me.

'Yes, we have one down the hall, follow me.' the further you walked into the stables the less fresh air there was and the more dust I breathed in. I tried my utter best not to cough as I followed the man to the last stable.

The horse that filled the stable was brown with white spots. It was small but postured well. I thought. I had thick black manes.

'It's a little small but it's strong, I'm telling you. This one will be able to take you to Rome, no doubt.' He said. I was sure that the man wasn't telling the whole truth. But I didn't know enough about horses to tell him he was wrong.

'How long will it take me to reach Rome?'

'I would say about a day or twelve. Give or take. He will have to rest in between riding. Make sure he has plenty of grass to eat and water to drink.' he said as he flicked his wrist to some of the other workers who started saddling the horse up. It was ready within a minute. 'It'll cost 30 lire.' he said turning around to look at me. I was shocked at the amount of money he asked. But I didn't argue with him. Servius had warned me that things would be more expensive for us. Servius had made sure that I would have enough money before he left. I could tell the man was surprised at the ease with which I had given him the money. I just wanted to get away from him as quickly as possible.

'It looks like a great horse, I'll take it.' I said as I gave the man his money. He had a rather troubled look on his face but didn't say anything to me. Afraid that he would see the fear in my eyes I looked at the ground rather than the horse, as it was being taken out of its stable. I had never gotten this close to a horse before and it got to me that this was a living creature. One that could do what he wanted without me being able to stop him. I had no idea how I would keep it under control. But that was something I would figure out once I was far away from this stable.

The man offered the reigns of the horse to me. I took them, unsure of how to hold them properly. I hoped that I looked confident and sure of what I was doing. The man didn't look at me or say anything.

And so I turned around, ready to leave the stable. Nobody held me back and I wasn't going to look back at them. The only thing I heard them say, as I left the stable was "Let's hope he doesn't sicken the horse" which was applauded by a wave of laughter.

CHAPTER 9

The beginning of the road to Rome was filled with farms that circled themselves around the city of Venice. There were plants growing as far as the horizon stretched. There were little animals, however. Something I found quite relieving because I wasn't sure how the horse would respond to them. Its big muscular body moved underneath me. It hadn't been as difficult as I expected to get on his back. I tightly held onto the reigns, scared that the horse would run back home the moment I let go of them. Back to its beloved stable, where all his friends were and where there was enough food to eat. Its hoofs on a ground filled with straw.

Up on the back of a horse that I had never seen before, all I longed for was home. Going back to Poveglia. Being with Servius. Sure, the days at Poveglia were miserable, filled with death. But at least I wasn't alone. With Servius by my side, everything would be okay. He would tell me what to do, over and over again until I finally understood. His soft but stern voice would speak to me.

Out here there was freedom. Freedom to go wherever I wanted to. To be who I wanted to. Opportunities beyond the little island. A place filled with so much room to go felt so empty to me. My thoughts were the only thing here to fill up the void.

With so much time to think, with so many things to think of, my brain kept going back to Servius. He was really dead. He was now in the company of many ghosts whom he had tried to help. Who's lived he had tried to save but had failed. Would he be happy alongside them? Would he enjoy the company of the ghosts?

Would he enjoy their company more than mine?

The road I was following was made out of stone. It was easy to see and therefore easy to ride. The horse understood this as well, as I barely had to tell him where to go. Once the stone streets made way for the dirt paths, trouble started to arise.

The hooves on the ground made the same noise as Servius's boots made on Poveglia. Servius was walking in front of me. Making his way through the thick layer of plants that had taken over Poveglia. I had trouble keeping up while Servius made big strides forward. "Servius! Servius! Please wait!" I yelled but he didn't slow down. I tried to catch up with him but no matter how hard I tried it didn't matter. The figure got smaller with the minute and dissolved into the horizon, leaving me alone on the empty island.

I was shocked out of the dream, desperately trying to find my balance on the back of the horse, who had figured out his own path to walk. I clenched the saddle, and the horse shifted its weight to the other side, getting me back in the saddle. It wasn't the first time I had almost fallen off. Riding a horse was costing way more energy than I had thought. The more tired I became the more I let the horse decide where it went and when it wanted to stop. I let him drink whenever he wanted to drink and eat whenever he wanted to eat. This however made that I would sit on its back for many hours at a time. The horse had more energy than I had and so I found myself dozing off now and then.

After a few days, the houses that filled the lands were slowly fading into the background. Only the grass and the bright blue horizon are there to keep me company. And the horse of course. Who seemed to be getting tired, slowing down his pace.

The slowed-down motion of the horse gave me some room to breathe. I loosened the grip of my right hand around the reigns. I reached down behind to feel if the plague mask was still bound to the saddle of the horse. My hands quickly found it. It was still tightly bound. I had reached my hand backward every five minutes or so. Making sure that I hadn't lost it. It had been there every time. It was not like I wouldn't hear it if the mask fell from the saddle, I wanted to prevent that from happening. Not knowing whether I would ever need to use the mask again. If I had to, I preferred it to be in one piece.

Next, my hand reached inside my thick cloak. My fingers traced the outline of the bottle. Making sure the cap was still on it and it hadn't broken. The motions of the horse were often sudden but had never been so bad that the bottle had broken. The ring was still on my finger and the suitcase was still bound to the side of the saddle. Servius was still with me. My hand took back the grip on the reigns.

The horse shot to the right. I lost my balance for a moment but caught myself before I fell out of the saddle. I had been stiff from all the riding, and the sudden movement made paint shoot through my entire body. The horse had stopped walking. Standing still beside the dirt path. My heart was beating out of my chest. I let one hand go of the reigns after a little while. I pat the horse on his neck, hoping that would calm him down a little. It didn't. The horse shot forward and to the left, throwing me off its back.

I fell on the hard ground, hearing a loud crack. My heart stopped. My hand reached into my cloak but found the bottle was still in one piece. I spun my head to the road, where I saw that the mask had fallen off. I could see the horse continue running away in the distance, but that didn't worry me. I stood up as quickly as I could, trying not to grunt as my body was aching with every move I made. I looked around me in one clean motion. There was no one to see on the horizon.

I raced towards the fallen mask. Trying not to show any sign of being scared, even though there was no one around me who could judge. Servius had told me the most important thing was to hide any sign of being vulnerable. Even from oneself. "They will catch on to it. They will know that the choices you make at that moment are formed by emotions. They'll make use of it." he had repeated many times.

The mask was still in one piece. The crack that I heard had come from one of the glasses. It had shattered from the impact when it had hit the ground. When I put it on I could see the star, fading the view from my left eye. I took it off and looked around me once more, but there was still no one.

I held the mask close to me as I started walking towards the horse. My head shifted from right to left, trying to figure out what had scared the horse. Something that didn't really matter to me. My heart was racing. Still scared that I would lose Servius once more. That I would truly lose him this time.

My grasp was strong, too strong. There was a slight dent in the mask when I had finally caught up with the horse. I took back the reigns and patted the horse on his neck. The horse however had all forgotten about what had scared him and was peacefully eating grass. I raised myself back in the saddle. My eyes daunted around, but the field was as normal. Only the blue sky had seen what had happened. And the horse of course.

Servius would have been embarrassed if he saw what had happened. Sitting, shaking in the saddle, eyes darting all around the place, with dirt smeared on my face. My lack of concentration on my surroundings that had led me to hitting the ground. I had failed him. He was still in one piece but his view of me wouldn't be.

He would have never made this mistake. The only thing I had shown him was my inability to follow his wise words.

I set the horse to walking. Trying to leave my place of shame behind. Blinding the sky from the truth. A truth that was already losing its original shape in my brain. Only keeping the form that I had wanted it to be. With only the ghost of my master to tell me I was lying.

CHAPTER 10

The countryside soon found itself changed into a deep forest. The trees rose high above me, even though I was on a horse. Now and then there were animals crossing the path. Nothing dangerous, luckily. I had only the horse to protect me. Who didn't seem to be bothered by the animals scurrying near his feet. I didn't even dare to think of what he would do when an enemy showed up from behind the flowers. I knew then, that I would be on my own.

I opened up the map and tried to figure out where I was. I had only a small bottle of ink to write with, something that had turned out to be impossible on a horse, even when it stood still. Therefore I could not fill in on the map what paths I had taken, and thereby figure out where I would have to go next.

Servius had taught me a little about geography, but never much about detailed maps. Besides the one of Poveglia, which didn't help me now. Although I had never seen a map this detailed and big, I had a good idea of where I had been. Up until now.

I seemed to go uphill a bit, but the map didn't show any indication of heights. I stopped the horse, or at least, I tried to get the horse to stop. It took about 20 meters before the horse actually stopped and I dismounted. I held onto the reigns with my left hand.

With the map in one hand and the horse in the other, I looked around me. The sun was sinking down and the coolness of the evening began to settle in. Without any light, it would be impossible to read the map. I took off a robe that was bound to the other side of the saddle. Fastening one end to a thin tree, and the other end to the horse. Once it was certain that the horse couldn't run away I started gathering some sticks to build a fire. I threw all the sticks I found on top of one another. Leaving enough space in between where the fire would be and the bushes. The last thing I wanted was to set the forest on fire.

I started a small fire, just big and bright enough for me to read the map next to. I held the map dangerously close to the fire. It didn't take long before the flames had bound themselves to the corner of the paper. I let out a small cry and hit the corner with my hand, stopping the fire from taking any more of the map.

'You seem like a real professional.' A voice said, coming from the darkness. The voice carried a rather French accent. Two man riding horses, that were at least twice the size as the horse that I was riding, made their way to me. Both men and the horses were dressed in heavy armour. The other man didn't say anything but simply laughed at the other man's remark. I squinted my eyes, hoping they would adjust so that I could more clearly see the figures that were standing on the other side of the fire.

'At least I look like I'm used to camping outside.' I mocked weakly. Mocking clearly wasn't something they were all too familiar with.

'I wouldn't make fun of us like that ever again, as it will be the last thing you do.' The men got out of their saddles, making their way to the other side of the campfire. Where I was sitting uncomfortably on the ground. They seemed a lot taller now that they were standing in the light and I could finally see them. They were looking down at me. Their eyes searched the ground around me. I quickly shoved the plague mask behind me, trying to hide it from their view. It was no use, as they had already seen it. They shared a quick look with one another. 'Luckily death seems to be something you're quite intimate with already.' I was starting to get annoyed by the men standing in front of me, but cautious to say anything else. Slightly worried about what they would do if I offended them once more. But it couldn't simply do nothing. The calming voice of Servius was filling my brain as I took the mask and placed it on my lap. My frustrations wouldn't help me in this situation, and neither would trying to hide who I was. It was best that I took pride in it, showing I was certain of who I was.

'It would be a great honour to bury your bodies, gentlemen; but that life I've left behind.' The men chuckled at this. Lowering themselves, holding up their hands to warm them by the fire.

'The mask reflects something different.' the more talkative man said. There was a shimmer of curiosity showing in his eyes. 'If you've truly left behind that life, then why carry that mask?' I waited before responding. Pondering over the question the man had just asked. I wasn't all too sure that I had an answer to that.

'I carry this mask with me to remember someone.' my voice lowered itself into a gloomy drone. 'Someone I lost.'

'Did you care about that person?'

'Care.' The other man spitted out in a half laugh. I had come to notice that he was the less talkative one. Hiding behind the other man, watching what was happening in front of him from a safe distance. I could tell by the way he looked at the other man that he stood lower in ranking. He didn't seem to care about it, neither did the other guy. Who seemed happy to take all responsibility.

'He has a point.' The other man said. I gave him a confused look because I hadn't come to the point the other man had supposedly just made. 'If you care so much about that person that you carry around the mask, something that scares off everyone around you, why do it at all?' This was a question I had not seen coming, nor that I completely understood. The man seemed to notice and explained himself further. 'If you care about someone that much, why be scared to forget her?'

'Him.'

'Then why be scared to forget him.' At first glance, both men hadn't looked all that intelligent. Getting through life by using the muscles they had gained rather than thinking. But that was something I had been wrong about.

'I'm not scared to forget him.'

'Then why carry the mask? If you're not scared to forget him, then why hold on to something that causes nothing but trouble, just because you lost someone.'

'I would like to think he wants me to keep the mask with me. That he can be with me through the mask.'

'That's one asking ghost.' The man laughed. Neither I nor the other guy joined him. My eyes were fixed on him, he didn't seem all too worried that I didn't laugh. 'It's a good thing we didn't kill you. You make great company my friend. Where are you headed.' he said, giving me a pat on my shoulder. I looked into the fire, having to decide whether or not to tell him the truth.

'Rome.' Everything in me screamed not to trust these men. Servius wouldn't have trusted them. He would have scared them away. He would have shown them that whom they were talking to was more dangerous than they were. Everything I could do was accept their appearance, besides, I had no idea how I would get myself to Rome. These men could very well be my best luck in getting there.

'How fortunate! That's where we're headed too.' the silent man bellowed. 'You should ride with us. We were planning on continuing on first light. You better get some rest. If the ghost won't haunt you!' Both men seemed to think that what pretty funny. I didn't. But I laughed anyways and decided that it was better not to take any chances of pissing them off. After all, I had just found my way to Rome.

* * *

When the first light rose, the men were already up and about. The morning air was chilly. The fire that had kept me warm throughout the night had burned out. Though the ambers were still glistening red. I held my hands close to them for a little while, trying to steal as much warmth away from what was left.

The men didn't greet me as I gathered all my stuff together, which wasn't much, and brought them over to my horse. The horse was still bound to the same tree. His head hung low and he had his eyes closed. I felt bad for having to wake him at such an early hour, but the men were almost ready to go and I didn't want them having to wait for me.

'Where did you find a horse like that?' The leader of the two asked. The tone of his voice made clear that it wasn't a compliment.

'I got him at a stable just outside Venice. They told me it was a fine horse.' The man looked at me with big eyes. 'But I don't know that much about horses.' I quickly added. The man nodded his head strongly.

'Well, I'm afraid they lied to you.' Once again the men laughed. I wondered what it must feel like to consider everything that is being said as funny. It surely wasn't funny to me. It didn't bother me much that the horse wasn't the finest out there. He had brought me here and had done it without much trouble.

It didn't take long before everyone was ready, climbing in their saddles. Something that took me a great effort as I was stiff from the days before. We started the ride for the day. The silent man rode behind me as I filled the place next to the other man. The hooves of the horses made a soft rhythm in the background. The uniforms that the men were wearing were squeaking with each movement they made.

'I don't think I caught your names.' I said, hoping the talking would be loud enough to wash away the sound of their uniforms.

'My name is Jean. This man behind me is Pierre. And what do they call you?'

'Fransisco.' A grin grew on Jean's face. Of course, that was funny to them.

'Nice name.' Jean said.

'Thank you.' I said. It was answered by a long silence. The man didn't seem too annoyed that I started to talk, and walking in silence soon became boring, so I decided to try once more. 'You're from France.'

'What gave it away?'

'Your accents.' I looked over to Jean. He grinned.

'Really? I thought our uniforms might have given it away more clearly.' he answered. I hadn't given their uniforms a good look before, but now in the daylight, it was very clear that they were French. 'I don't suppose you speak French?' Jean asked.

'No.' Quickly escaped my lips. This was a lie of course. Servius had given me many lessons in French, which I hadn't forgotten over the years. I was as good at it as I was at walking.

'If you're French, then what are you doing here?'

'We're taking over this land, my friend. Napoleon needs it more than you do. I'm lucky to be here. You wouldn't want to be in Paris nowadays.'

'Why not?' I asked. Jean grew silent. He didn't seem all too comfortable to talk about it. But Pierre who was still riding behind us didn't seem as worried and started to explain.

'There are a lot of…' the man behind started. His Italian wasn't as good as the Jean's. It took him a while to figure out how to continue. '…protests, fights. They don't like the new reign. For many, he has had his great years. It's not safe there.'

'We have already taken over Rome. It is not so bad there.' Jean added. 'Of course, there are soldiers all around, but no one who goes there is in real danger.'

'What's so bad about Napoleon?'

'Well, the size of his ignorance for starters.' Pierre spit out. Jean looked around them nervously.

'He's quite the idiot as well.' Jean whispered. 'My guess is that he won't last another year without someone taking his life.' Pierre nodded at this. I wasn't all that well informed about Napoleon. I worried that he would cause a problem on my travels, but knowing there was nothing I could do about it now, I focused on the landscape around me. Even though every muscle in my body was aching from the days in the saddle I was enjoying the travels. Poveglia wasn't all too ugly, but it was nothing compared to the view around me now. 'So what's your deal?' Jean asked after a while.

'I'm sorry?'

'Where are you from? What have you done with your life?'

'I grew up on Poveglia-,'

'What?' Jean interrupted me.

'Poveglia is a quarantine island. It is located between Venice and Lido. They brought people with the plague there, to keep them away from the rest.'

'And you grew up there? Does that mean you have the plague?' Jean asked. There was a slight fear glooming over his face.

'No, no.' I said quickly. 'My father was a doctor there. My mother was never around, and so I grew up there. Later I became a doctor myself. But now that the plague is gone, I am no longer needed there.' Jean nodded.

'The mask. Is that your father's?'

'No. That is mine.'

'But do you keep it to keep him with you?' Jean asked carefully.

'No.' I paused for a moment. The sudden reminder of Servius hurt more than I had expected it to. Jean seemed to notice and didn't push on. But I couldn't just leave it at that. I couldn't be scared to talk about Servius. 'When I grew up I wasn't all that close to my father. There was another doctor there, the head of the island. His name was Servius. He taught me everything I now know. He stood next to me when I needed him most. He died two years ago. The plague got hold of him. It's him who I'm carrying with me. When he died I promised that I would take his ashes to his wife. But I can't do that on why own. I need him by my side.'

'That's what brings you to Rome?' Jean spoke softly.

'Yes.' I said, keeping my eyes on the road. Not daring to look at either one of them.

Our conversation had dimmed down the energy amongst us. We rode for hours in silence, until the sun began setting. The soldiers were clearly used to riding for long hours. My legs were hurting and stiff. It took me a great amount of effort to get myself off the horse once we finally stopped. The soldiers had their backs turned to me when I stumbled out of the saddle. Almost falling over onto the ground.

We made a small fire together and sat around it. I lay down, closing my eyes to sleep as Jean and Pierre continued to talk. They soon changed their conversation to French. I forced myself to stay awake to listen to them. They lowered their voice, although I had told them that I didn't speak French. Maybe they hadn't believed me.

'We're getting close to Rome now. We will leave him around about a hundred kilometers away from the city.'

'Won't he get lost?' Pierre asked.

'No. We'll show him the route he has to take on his half-burned map. Besides, it's mostly one long road he has to follow. There will be no way that he will be lost.'

'Then why would we leave him.'

'It might be dangerous if they saw us with someone from Italy. That could get both us and him in a great amount of trouble.' Jean said.

'I understand.' Pierre answered. I understood too. I had never met this Napoleon, but he didn't seem all too great. And getting in trouble wasn't something I was looking forward to. I realised that I was very lucky to have met them. They had been extremely kind and weren't just going to leave me behind. They would do everything they could to make sure I would find my way to Rome.

And so a couple of days later we parted ways. They had shown me the way on my map as they had said they would. They even told me about their concerns if we were to continue to travel together. I did not make an issue out of it, quite the contrary, I thanked them for everything. They had truly saved me from being forever lost in the forest.

After we said our last goodbyes their horses shot forward. I had quite the trouble keeping my horse from following them. I tightened my legs around the horse and tugged a little on the reins. The horse wasn't too happy with it but it didn't run after them. Servius would have found it very funny that I had such great difficulty making the horse listen to me. Just seeing me on a horse would have been enough for him to laugh at me. I waited for over an hour before I started my way, making sure there was enough distance between me and the soldiers.

The last of the way to Rome was nothing more than following straight stone roads. When the walls of Rome came nearer there were loads of people about. There were wagons, pulled by horses, filling the road. There were people on horses riding about. Most of them were soldiers, like Jean and Pierre. Whom I didn't see. There were farms surrounding the city where plants were growing greatly.

CHAPTER 11

Rome was big, way bigger than Venice. Rome was filled with houses that each showed the individual but all together showed the history of the old Greeks. It didn't have the sea roaming through the city. There wasn't a boat to be seen. Only people. Italians as well as French scurried on the streets. Though most of the people appeared to be French.

French soldiers could be found on every corner. Leaning against the building, talking amongst themselves while scanning the streets. Though they didn't seem all too scary, nobody looked them in the eyes. Heads hanging low as they passed the soldiers. Believing that if they didn't see them then perhaps it meant they didn't exist. The men had their grip loosely around a gun. Holding them close, ready to use them if necessary. The look in their eyes didn't quite match the physical representation.

They were all standing in little groups, talking and laughing. Having normal conversations. Like they were at home sitting around a large table, each with a drink in their hands. They didn't seem all too worried. Lost in a world in which nothing seemed to happen.

I stood at the side of the road, a good bit away from them and observed them for a while. There was a group of kids that ran up to them. They were chatting loudly, but the sound didn't reach me clearly enough to understand what they were saying. The men looked at each other, seeming to hesitate. Then one of the men nodded and handed his gun to one of the little boys. Their greedy hands moved to the weapon. They soon had ripped it out of the soldier's hand and were running around the street with it, pretending to shoot people. The soldiers didn't seem to care much as they were back to talking and laughing. The rest of the children played along to the little game. Pretending to get shot and then lay on the ground as to be dead.

It made me sick looking at it. It wasn't a problem that they didn't seem all too bothered by death. But it wasn't something fun. Even kids should know that.

It wasn't going to help if I kept pondering, so I continued my way. Leading the horse to one of the nearby stables. It was placed just outside the city. In comparison to the stable in Venice, this one was the definition of clean. The stable was also about twice the size of the one in Venice. When I entered there were horses and people everywhere.

'Good morning?' I asked rather than said.

'Hello!' Jolted a set man that appeared from behind a horse. He looked eagerly at my horse like it was food rather than I living creature.

'Is there any chance I could get a stable for this horse.' I said pointing to the horse that stood beside me. I didn't look the man in the eyes as I talked. My eyes were more focused on all the things that were happening behind the man. It all looked like a perfectly organised mess. There were a few boys mucking out stables, whilst making fun of each other. Horses were taken from stables and put in stables. There was someone carrying a large bale of hay whilst making his way through the madness. At the end of the stable, there was a small group of women, standing very close to one another. Now and then they would turn around to make sure no one was listening to them. They were talking softly and seemed to be giggling. They could have been talking about anything, horses, men, or murder.

'You're a funny man!' The set man screamed with laughter. 'Of course, there is! There are plenty of stables at the end that are big enough for your horse.' The man turned around but stopped quickly, turning back towards me. 'It'll cost of course!' He laughed.

'Of course.' I answered, not feeling all too comfortable in this place. The man took over the reins of my horse. I was glad he did, as I had taken the plague mask from the saddle before I walked into the stables. I was now holding it with both hands, having it turned in such a way that it would directly be obvious what I was carrying.

'Good, good! Where are you from; if I may ask?' The man said as he almost ran to the other side of the stables.

'Venice.'

'Ah, Venice! You've traveled quite a distance, haven't you? This horse must be tired. How long did it take, 10 days?' The man asked, slowing his run down to a slow shuffle.

'Around 16.' I answered. I wasn't sure if it had actually been 16 days, as from the fourth day on I hadn't bothered keeping track.

'That's quite the trip! Did you do it all by yourself?'

'Yes, just me and the horse.' I said. Thinking about Jean and Pierre. 'And Servius.' I whispered after it.

'Who!?' The man almost shouted.

'No one.' My eyes darted around me. The man had surely heard the name, but I wasn't about to tell him the truth. 'Just my dog. He died.'

'That's a shame.' I said. Feeling rather a bit guilty that I called Servius a dog. 'That thing you're carrying, is that yours?' The man asked, nodding his head towards the mask. If the man was just as excited about walking as he was talking we would have reached the end of the stable In four seconds. But the man shuffled his way down the stables. His steps were smaller than the smallest mouse I had ever seen.

'Yes, it is mine.'

'How did you get it?'

'I used to be a doctor.' The man now stopped walking altogether.

'A doctor? I know plenty of doctors, who taught you?'

'Servius.' The man shook his head.

'I don't know that one.'

'Well, he's dead now anyways.'

'I would say that you should be used to death. But I don't think you can really get used to losing someone. But you might just know how to handle it better. My condolences.'

'Thank you.' I replied. My voice sounded distant, looking at the broken glass of the mask.

'This one will do!.' The man said as he turned left, leading the horse into the smallest stable that I had ever seen. The horse turned around in the stable, touching every wall as he did so. 'He looks very happy with it, doesn't he?' the man beamed as the horse looked everything but happy. But I did not say this to the man. I walked into the stall, barely getting myself in between the horse and the wall. If the horse was spooked by anything I would turn into some mush stuck to the side. I struggled as I took the suitcase and saddle from the horse's back. The hairs that were underneath the saddle were pressed flat and soaked in sweat.

'He sure does look happy.' I said as I carried the saddle out of the stable. 'How much will it be to keep him here?'

'One lira per four days, that is if you feed him yourself. If you don't it will be one lira per two days.' I told him I would go for the two-day option and gave him a lira. The man wanted to hurry off but I stopped him before he could.

'Would you know any cheap place where I could sleep?'

'Of course! There's a little inn that is really cheap. Outside the stable, you go to the right. Then keep walking into the second street left. There is a little place, what is it called, sheep, sheep something, something with sheep. It's cheap but it's not much.'

'Thank you.' I said. The man had already forgotten me as I walked outside of the stable. As I went to find a place to sleep that wasn't much better than the stable my horse was in now.

Outside the sun was shining brightly and the heat got to me quickly. My cloak, which covered most of my body, was completely black. With the sun shining on it it felt like I was being cooked alive. I opened up the cloak, letting the light breeze flow through it. I shifted the mask to my right arm, so I could move the left more freely. Once it felt good again, I picked up the suitcase and continued once more.

Both the street to the left and the street to the right were filled with people. There were carriages in the middle trying to get through, shouting at people who walked in their way. Voices were covering the sound the birds made as they flew over. The streets were made of stones that were broken on too many places to count. My feet shot away one stone after another as I made my way down the street. When I took the second street left it felt like I had just entered a cemetery. The street was completely empty, except for a lost dog, who was trying to find leftover food in the gutters. Its paws were covered in dirt and the creature was slender. The silence bounced off the building. The whole street had an eerie feeling to it.

I felt bad for walking past the dog, but I had no idea how to take care of it. Servius would have known. Servius would also have told me to leave it alone. That this creature's fate was to be here, starving on the streets. That I should leave it be his life, and not make it my own. Servius had never really believed in fate. He didn't even believe one's life had a path. He believed that life was just a continuous line of actions. That the only thing that mattered was the action that was currently happening: the choice that you made at the moment. The rest would come later. In the end, your life would tell its story, one that you chose to make, not one of the many that were laid out for you. But that didn't stop him from using the word fate. Whenever I asked too many questions or dragged on him to go along with something he often told me off. Telling me to focus on my own fate rather than his.

He just said that to shut me up of course. Fate was something I often thought about. Wondering if my fate was to be stuck on Poveglia forever. To stay there until I died. To have me come to an end there just like Servius had. But that had changed. For now.

I walked past the dog. Making a promise to myself that I would get food somewhere to give to it. A promise I knew I probably wasn't going to keep. Some part of me though hoped that the thought of a promise was enough for me to actually do it. Only time would tell me if that was true.

CHAPTER 12

The little inn, as the man had said, didn't look all too good. The whole building seemed to lean a bit forward and all together the building looked abandoned. The door was too small for its frame, and one of the windows was broken. There was a place where the sign should have hung, right above the door. But the sign lay flat on the ground. A few bricks were missing here and there. There was no light shining from inside. But all in all, it didn't seem like the building would collapse today and so I entered.

The door creaked as I opened it, a sound that I had grown quite used to on Poveglia. There was a little bell hanging above the door which it should have hit but didn't because the door was too small. So only the creaking told someone that I had entered the building. I walked into the small space that was filled with a few chairs, a few tables, and a bar. There were only two people in the room. There was one sitting at the bar, his back to me, and a hooded figure that sat in the corner of the room. I walked over to the bar, taking in the inside of the building.

'What may I do for you sir?' the man groaned. He hadn't turned around to look at me.

'Could I get a room?' I asked. The man turned to me. He was looking me up and down and noticed the plague mask that I was holding in my left hand. I quickly tried to hide it behind my body but he had already shot up from his chair. Quickly making his way behind the bar so to create distance between me and him. His face changed and I wasn't so sure anymore that I could get a room here.

'A room for... one?' the man asked. It seemed obvious to me that I was asking for a room for one. There was no one with me.

'Yes please.' I answered. The hooded figure that sat in the corner of the room hadn't moved, but I knew that he had been listening to our conversation. He was looking our way and had stopped drinking so to be sure that he would be able to hear every word that we said. He didn't seem all too happy with me here. I had grown used to that. As a plague doctor people feared you. I couldn't blame them. They barely knew anything about who we were and what we did. The only thing that goes around in their mind is that we are associated with the plague, with death.

'Lucky you, lucky you. I have one room left.' the man said. I wondered if the man only had one room, as there didn't seem to be many guests about. 'For how many nights would you like to stay?'

'Two, if that's possible.'

'Yes of course. May I have your name?' the man opened a big book that lay in front of him and took a pen ready to write my name down. I was pleasantly surprised that the man hadn't sent me away.

'Fransisco Festus.' I answered. The man who had seemed so ready to write my name stopped. He looked at me his eyes big. The hooded figure shifted in his chair. The man nodded and quickly wrote down my name. I didn't know why the man was so taken aback by my name.

'That will be one lira please.' It wasn't as much as I expected. I put my suitcase down, not daring to let go of the mask. I put my hand in the pocket of my cloak and took out a little bag. It was tightly closed by a string that could easily be removed. I searched around in the little bag until I found a lira. I stretched my hand out to give it to the man. Halfway I decided to put the coin on the bar, as the man behind it probably wouldn't want to touch my hand. He quickly took it, his hand full of greed. 'Thank you.' the man muttered. It didn't take him long to pick up a key and place it on the exact spot where I had laid my coin. I picked up the key. It was engraved with the number eight on it. So he had more than one room here. 'That is your room number.' the man said. 'The stairs are on the right, just behind that door.' the man said pointing to the other side of the room. The door that he pointed at looked a lot better than the front door had looked. This one is the proper size for its frame. 'Go up and then at the end of the hallway.'. I gave him a little nod, picked up my suitcase, and made my way to the door and up the stairs.

The hallway upstairs was just as gloomy as the room below. Room eight was the room at the end of the hallway, just like the man had said. The door to the room stood a few meters further away than the doors of the other rooms were. I opened the door to the room. A weird smell entered my nostrils. Making it so that I couldn't breathe for a second. The room was filled with nothing more than a bed, a wardrobe, and a tub of water. There weren't any rats scurrying around and everything seemed to be dry. It was more than I could have hoped for from what the outside of the building had told me. I placed my suitcase on the floor and put down the mask on the bed. I sat down next to it, the bed creaked under my weight. I checked the pocket of my cloak. The bottle was still in one piece. Servius was still un-broken.

CHAPTER 13

'Over here.' Servius said as he led him over the little bridge that connected the main part of the island with the burning grounds. Fransisco had never been here this early on in the morning. The sun slowly starts to rise from the horizon. Giving just enough light for Servius and Fransisco to see where they were going. Servius had told Fransisco to get up early but did not share with him why. Fransisco had done as Servius asked. Silently creeping to the other side of the island, while not being seen by anyone.

'What are we doing here?' Fransisco asked Servius. Servius did not answer. He let the way through the thick bushes. Multiple thorns biting into the side of Fransisco's legs. Though he didn't complain. 'Servius?' Fransisco started but decided against it. It did not take long before Servius stopped.

'We're here.' he simply said. Fransisco looked around him. They were standing in the middle of multiple types of plants. He wasn't sure why Servius had taken him here. Servius did not explain, which frustrated Fransisco a little. Instead of explaining he simply looked at Fransisco and smiled.

'Why did you take me here?' Fransisco asked after they had stood there in silence for what felt like minutes.

'What do you see?' Servius asked. Being more sceptical than he usually was.

'Plants.' Fransisco said. Servius didn't like the answer he had gotten and grunted.

'Yes. But there is something here today that wasn't here before.' Fransisco looked at him with glassy eyes. Servius gave him a cheering nod, but that did not help Fransisco understand.

'I'm afraid you're going to have to give me a hint Servius.' Servius nodded but didn't seem very happy with it.

'I'm afraid a hint won't do you any good.' he said, which Fransisco took a little personal. 'Look up, in the trees.' Fransisco did as Servius asked but didn't see anything new. 'The figs.' Servius said, noticing that he had to state it even more clearly. 'You really aren't awake yet, are you?' he said after Fransisco had simply nodded at the remark of the figs.

'What is so important about the figs?' Fransisco asked. Servius reached his hand up to the tree. Grabbing hold of a fig and pulling it from the tree. He held the fig up in his hand, so Fransisco could have a good look at it.

'Try it.' Servius said. Fransisco looked at him like he was going crazy. 'Try it-,' he said again 'It won't kill you' Fransisco took the fig hesitantly. He slowly

brought it to its mouth, while keeping his eyes fixed on Servius. He didn't lose this gaze as he took a bite, which would have probably been a bit weird for Servius but Fransisco wanted to be sure he wasn't playing any games with him. But once Fransisco took a bite that worry left his mind. The rich taste of the fig filled his mouth. Servius was grinning at Fransisco's reaction. 'Nice, aren't they?'

'Yes, very.' Fransisco said with his mouth full. Servius reached for another fig, pulling it from the tree for him to eat. Together they stood in silence, enjoying their figs together, as the sun was making its way up the sky.

CHAPTER 14

The days turned into night and the night turned back into day. I had spent all my time in my little room in the inn. I had no idea of what I was going to do. I wasn't even sure there was a plan that I could follow. I was going to the pawn shop, that much I knew. I was looking for Maximilien Robespierre. Someone I had never seen nor heard anything about and whom I wasn't at all familiar with. I didn't even know for sure if any of his work could be found in the pawn shop. If he was an artist at all. The wooden gourd that had traveled with me in the suitcase had made me believe that he could be an artist. It was the only thing so far that I had that could lead me to Servius's wife. If Servius had just told me who his wife was and where I could find her this would have gone a lot quicker. I should have asked him. I could have asked him. But I was so lost in the fear of losing him that I hadn't thought of it. And Servius had been too busy dying to tell me.

After his death, I had searched through many of the books kept of Poveglia. Trying to find Servius's name in one of them. Telling me where Servius was from and who his family was. But once I found his name none of that information had been there. His name stood there, in big bold letters, but underneath nothing but his date of birth was written down. I had found it very odd of course. I had pondered many hours about whom to ask but knew that no one on the island knew him as well as I did and they probably wouldn't have answers for me. At some point, I questioned if Servius had made up his wife. If the sickness had gotten to him so bad that he began believing things that weren't true. I quickly hushed away the little voice that had brought it up. Not believing that my master could have lost it.

I left my suitcase at the inn. As well as the wooden gourd. I had spent many hours the day before examining it, making sure that I knew every little detail there was to know. Taking it with me seemed like too much of a gamble for me. I picked up the mask and made sure that Servius's ashes were neatly tucked in my cloak. I locked the door and walked down the stairs. Stopping at the bar before leaving. The space behind the bar was empty. I looked around for a bit but couldn't find the man that had been there the day before. The hooded figure that sat in the corner of the room was still sitting in the same place as yesterday. Clearing my throat, I turned back around and waited for the owner of the inn to get back. Something that didn't take as long as I expected.

'Good morning. I have a question. Where can I find this building?' I asked the man as I slid the paper with the information of the pawn shop over to him.

'Good morning.' The grunted, clearly not very awake yet. 'That's in the center of the city. It's a big building with many decorations on the outside. There flags start two streets from here. Just turn left outside and then the first right, then keep walking. You'll find them.' the man said.

'Thank you.' I said as I took the flyer. The man grunted something under his breath and walked off. I turned around heading for the door. The man in the corner turned his head, following me as I walked out the door, into the busy city.

Soon I found the air filled with flags. Each shows a different piece of art that would be displayed in the pawn shop. There were many people who stopped in front of the flags, looking up and talking to one another about what they saw. Telling each other what they liked and disliked about it. I wondered how many of them would have already been sold.

Without knowing I turned the mask a little upwards, like I was showing the art to Servius. Waiting to hear his thoughts about everything displayed. I followed the flags until the big building revealed itself. The outside of the building was decorated with so many flags that the building was almost completely covered. The parts of the building that weren't covered revealed engravings in the stone. Many different patterns circled the building. There were big statues near the front doors, reaching just a little higher than the first floor. Behind these statues were pillars hidden that kept up part of the building. I could barely see the front doors behind all the people trying to find their way inside.

Most people took a step back as I marched forward towards the door. The people around me fell silent, as they watched me walk past them, inside the building. Their silent stares were burning into my skin even though most of it was covered by my cloak. The way up to the door was made clear. Everyone had cleared the way, each one of them just as scared to get near me. The doors were open as I walked through them. The moment I crossed the line from outside to inside whispering started behind me. The people on the inside on the other hand didn't seem to notice me at all. Each one of them to busy with the pieces of art all around them to even worry about anyone but themselves.

I stepped in a line to buy a ticket. There was some space left between me and the person in front of me. Scared that they wouldn't want me to get too close I kept my distance. Scared of their reaction if even just an inch of me was in their personal space. All that I was trying to do was prevent being thrown out. As it was my turn to buy a ticket the person behind the desk didn't greet me the way he had others. His big eyes were darting around, trying to find help.

'I would like one ticket please.' I said, hoping that the calmness in my voice would transport over to him. He answered with the prize which I quickly handed over to him. His hands were shaking as he handed me the ticket. 'Have a nice day.' I said as it became clear that he wouldn't and quickly walked away.

I walked into the crowded hallway. There were big chandeliers hanging from the ceiling every few meters. They were made of glass and were shining rainbows around the room from the shining sun. The sun came into the room through the large windows that filled most of the left wall. The windows had painted glass on the top of them, each showing a different picture. The walls were painted red and white with gold details on them. There were paintings hanging all around the room. I hadn't even reached the room that I was looking for but I had already seen more artwork than I had in my entire life.

I had never seen real art. If you could call it that. There weren't any artworks on Poveglia. And the few years before I got to Poveglia were scraped away from my memory.

Poveglia was all I knew. The grey walls, the lack of decoration. Trees and plants around the walls and most of the building were covered in dirt.

This was different. This was cheerful. The paintings hanging in this room were colourful. Every inch of each canvas was filled. There were paintings with people in them and paintings without. Great landscapes towering over the small people in the foreground. The skies were the bluest I had ever seen. There was everything here. Everything I had never seen.

I found one painting I liked in particular. There was no human, just a sea, in which peacefully sailed a large ship. The sea reminded me of the one by Poveglia. The big ships sailed towards the little island. As I started at the painting the room around me began to change. The wall behind the painting turned grey. The murmuring of people disappeared. I looked around me wondering where everyone had gone. All four walls were solid, without any windows. The hallway seemed to be a lot more narrow than it had been before. All the paintings had disappeared. I turned around and around unsure of where to go when all of a sudden a figure stood at the end of the hallway.

He was standing there, looking at me. He had taken his plague mask off and was holding it in front of his body using two hands to keep it up. He was wearing his cloak, which seemed to be drenched. Water dripped on the floor underneath him.

'Servius!' I shouted, not knowing that everyone in the hallway, the ones that stuck to real life, could hear me. There he was. Standing only a few meters away from me, but it seemed so far. I tried to walk, to make my legs take me to him; but I couldn't. I wanted to get to him. To feel his presence close to me. I shouted and shouted, trying to get his attention but he didn't react to me.

I tried to take a step once more, my body moving its weight between my two legs. But nothing happened. I was stuck in my spot. I didn't want him to leave, I didn't want to forget him.

'Fransisco.' a voice said. A voice that didn't belong to Servius. Servius's voice was gloomy. This voice was bright. This voice was soft and caring. I didn't know this voice. I turned around, trying to find some hint as to where this voice was coming from. The room didn't change and there was no one around me. Servius was gone. This voice had made him disappear.

Then I felt it. There was a hand grasping my arm, dragging me out of the world I was lost in; back to reality. There it was. The face. The man behind the voice was standing next to me. He was about the same height as me, perhaps a little taller. He was wearing black clothing like me. He was holding my mask. One of the glasses was still broken but besides that, there wasn't any new damage. I eagerly looked at the mask, questioning how he dared take it from me. He saw this and quickly pushed the mask back into my hands.

'You dropped it.' the man said. His hair was short and black. He didn't have a full beard, but there were some hairs showing. His eyes were dark brown with a twinkle in them. He overall gave me a kind impression. 'Fransisco?' he said again. He noticed I was back to reality. I nodded. There was nothing left in my body that could do any different. He didn't let go of my arm. He looked around him. Embarrassment rose as I saw that everyone around us was silently staring at us. The man dragged me across the hallway. Not caring about the people that were looking at us; only caring about where he was going. We didn't have to try to get through the group of people. As soon as they saw us they cleared the way. Their disgusted faces were printed in my brain. This had been a look that many held and was all too familiar to me. I knew of course that all people would try their hardest to stay away from me. Servius had warned me. This also happened on Poveglia.

When there were boats passing through. But it had never been this bad. People have always looked at me with fear. The longer they stayed the lesser it got. Though a look of disgust wasn't the same. It felt more real. It hit me harder. Something that couldn't simply be erased by time.

The mysterious figure opened the door to the right of us. I hadn't noticed where he was going until I was in the room itself. It was a small broom closet. That is, small for this building. The size of the broom closet was about the same as the room in the inn. The entire floor and walls were covered in small tiles. There was a little light hanging from the ceiling. The entire room around us was filled with brooms and other such cleaning supplies. There wasn't any window in the room. It smelled rather fresh and it seemed like this room got the most cleaning of all. The more I realised how silent it was the more I began to think we weren't allowed to be in here.

'Who are you?' I asked. Looking the man dead in the eye, hoping to scare him a little.

'You don't recognise me?' he replied. I looked him up and down, trying to figure out what I should know him from. Did I ever meet him, had he ever been on Poveglia? Maybe he was the dark figure that sat at the corner of the inn. 'Has Servius never told you about me?' his voice was soft, almost sad. Sad because he had been forgotten, not important enough to be known. I tried to look him in the eyes but couldn't.

'He might have. I'm not sure. I don't think so, but maybe I've forgotten.'

'Don't sweat it. It doesn't really surprise me he hasn't told you about me.'

'Is that how you know my name?' only now did it occur to me that it was quite out of the ordinary that he had called me by my name.

'Yes, in a way. If I had never known Servius I wouldn't have known you. We've met before, when you were little. I took you from Rome to Venice. I don't want to sound like a cliché, but you've grown.' I didn't quite know how to respond to that. I looked at the mask in my hands. I traced my fingers over the broken glass. Stress flew over me, my heart skipping a beat. Reaching my hand in my cloak. The bottle was still in one piece. I nodded my head, unaware of the stranger's eyes looking at me. 'I saw you coming in on a horse yesterday.' he started. 'You seemed out of touch. I was waiting for Servius to come so I could greet you, be he didn't come. Did he send you out here alone? Did he say he would meet you here later?'

'No, no he didn't. I just thought I saw him.'

'That's alright.' he told me but his face was rather filled with worry. I couldn't blame him, as I was going completely insane.

'Maximilien.'

'Maximilien?'

'Yes, Maximilien Robespierre. The artist. I need to find him, he-,'

'As far as I know, he isn't an artist. And I believe that he is dead as well. What do you say we get out of here? Go back to my house. Go get something to drink. Then you'll tell me why Servius sent you here and you can ask as many questions as you wish, okay?' he asked, nodding his head as to answer himself. Servius hadn't sent me here. He didn't know that. My head nodded in reply before I could think. I had never met this man before and still didn't know his name, but he knew mine. He knew Servius. He had brought me to Venice? I didn't know if I could trust him, but I wanted to know his story. Hoping it would fill in the questions that I had.

CHAPTER 15

He led me all the way to the outer side of Rome. Where the buildings were smaller, and the houses had open fields behind them. There he opened the door of a little house, that stood in between two larger ones. The house was scarcely filled with decorations. A few paintings were hanging on the wall and there was just enough furniture filling the room to make it feel like someone actually lived here.

'Sit down.' the man said, waving his hand in the direction of an old sofa. It was broken in many places and rather small. Just big enough for two people to sit next to one another comfortably.

'Who are you? I asked one more realising he had never answered when I asked him the first time. I sat down on the sofa, which sagged dangerously low once I lowered my weight on it. I placed the mask on my lap.

'I'm Carlo. An old friend of Servius.' Carlo answered, throwing his cloak on one of the chairs that stood next to the sofa. Servius had never told me anything about him. I had never heard his name before, nor read it anywhere. It wasn't as Servius was one to tell about old friends, but still, I found it rather odd. If what he told me was true, that he brought me to Venice, he would have been important enough to name. 'Would you like something to drink?' Carlo asked.

'Some water will do.' I replied absently. Carlo walked away and returned back into the living room with two glasses of water. He placed them on the little table that stood in front of me and sat himself down on the sofa next to me.

'I guess you have many questions.' Carlo started after a long pause.

'I do.' I replied eagerly.

'Well, you better start asking then.' he smiled at me, encouraging me to ask. He looked like someone open to answer all questions. It was time to find out if that was actually true.

'When and where did you meet Servius.' I started. Unsure if this was the right question to ask first. Carlo scarped his throat.

'I met him quite some years ago.' Carlo started. 'I wouldn't be able to tell you the exact year though; sorry. I had exchanged many letters with him before I actually met him in Rome. After he got there from Paris.'

'Paris?' I asked surprised. Carlo shook his head.

'How much has Servius told you about his past?'

'Not much.' I confessed. Carlo looked at me with sorrow but didn't say anything about it. Which I silently thanked him for.

'He fled from Paris. Before you ask, I don't know the reason why. He wouldn't tell me. He had a lot of money and I needed it. He asked me to get him and you from Rome to Venice and find him a place to stay there; without anyone knowing about it. He told me he needed the time there to figure out the next step. You were also part of his plan. Again, I don't know how exactly. But he asked me to keep an eye on you in Venice, while he was figuring things out. Then he decided to go to an island near there, Poveglia, was it? He gave me the money, more than he said he would give me. He asked me to keep him informed of any news that came from France. And so I did. Did he send you here to deliver a message?' Carlo asked. His left eyebrow raised, seeming deep in thought. I looked at him, my hands stuck on the mask in my lap.

'He didn't send me here.' I said gloomy.

'You ran away?' Carlo guessed.

'No.' there was a puzzled look on his face. I knew I would have to explain that Servius had died eventually, but I was scared to speak the words out loud. So avoiding having to say it I began asking more questions. 'Did I come from Paris too?'

'I think so, yes.'

'Why did he go to Venice.'

'Not a clue.'

'Why Poveglia?'

'I'm not sure. But not many people go there. I think it was safest for him to go there. To keep him from being found.'

'Who were looking for him?'

'Again, I don't know. I'm really bad at answering these questions.' Carlo laughed. 'As I said, I don't know who he is, or what he is running from. I know he came from France and that he was rich. I do believe there were more people helping him get from one place to another. I don't know any names though.'

'What did he tell you about me?'

'He told me that you were very important. To keep you safe. He also told me that when the time was right you would come to me, to deliver a message.' Carlo said looking hopefully at me.

'He didn't tell me before he left.'

'He left Poveglia?' there it was. The moment I couldn't go around the truth. I had to tell him. I didn't want to say it. I hadn't talked about Servius's death with someone who had really known him. If I told him it would become real. He would be dead to both of us.

'He died.' Carlo nodded his head hanging it low. I took the glass that was filled with water and drank it all in one gulp. My hands were slightly shaking, and some of the water trailed down my chin. Trying to find anything to keep me from thinking of Servius. Telling Carlo that Servius was dead didn't really change a thing. He had been dead from the moment I had left Poveglia. That hadn't changed.

'That must have been it.' Carlo said.

'What?'

'The message you needed to send me. That he was dead.'

'Why would I have to tell you? And why didn't he tell me that when he was dying?'

'I had asked him many times who he was.' Carlo began. 'I wanted to know who I was dealing with, in case people would come threaten me, or try to kill me. He told me that he was important enough that his death would be noticed. Maybe that's not what he meant by it. Maybe I'm reading into it a bit too much. And for the dying. I don't think I would think about that were I dying. How did he die?'

'The plague caught him. It could have been. But why would he send me to tell you that, when you don't even know who he is?'

'No idea.' there was a long silence. A silence that could have been filled if Servius was here. Servius would have told us who he was. He wouldn't be able to keep it hidden if he were here. Told us who he was and who he was running from. Who he had tried to become. Perhaps he had become who he wanted to be; Servius. 'Did he tell you anything else?' Carlo's voice was slightly shaking. I didn't know it bothered him so much that Servius had died.

'He told me to get his ashes and ring back to his wife.' I said, Carlo nodded.

'Did he tell you who his wife was?'

'No?'

'Okay. That makes it a little tougher. Did he at least tell you where she could be found?'

'Also no. I have no idea who or where she is.'

'Then. What brings you here?' Carlo asked, looking at me. I sighed.

'The pawn shop. I found a wooden gourd with a bloody handkerchief inside, back on Poveglia. It belonged to Servius.

"Maximilien Robespierre" was carved into it. I thought maybe I could find him here.'

'I know that gourd. Someone sent it to me, telling me to give it to Servius. Which I did. Servius didn't want to tell me what it was about, but he paid me well, so I let it be. I do know that Maximilien is an advocate in Paris. Something with beheadings I believe.' There was a short silence hovering over the conversation. But of us deep in thought.

'So we have to go to Paris?' I spit out. Carlo shot up at this. His eyes questioned my sanity. I could tell that he wasn't all too pleased with that idea.

'I don't think that a good idea.'

'But there could be answers there!'

'Well yes, there could be answers there...'

'But?'

'Well, for starters, there is a lot going on in France right now. You know, with Napoleon and all. There are protests everywhere and those protests can become very dangerous. So going now, it's just not that good of an idea.'

'I don't see why not.'

'Don't you listen to me? I just explained why not.'

'Yes, it could be dangerous, so? Why should we wait? It could become worse if we wait. At least right now we know what is happening there, we are prepared. Besides, this can't wait. I have to get his ashes and ring to his wife. She can't just keep thinking her husband is alive, while he is laying in his grave.' my voice started to rise. There was buried down anger that I was carrying with me. 'We can't do that to him! If the roles were switched Servius would have already done it! I promised him I would do this!' Carlo took a few steps back. Noticing my anger, giving me the space I needed.

'This is about him, isn't it?'

'Who?'

'Servius of course.'

'Why would you say that?'

'I don't mean it in a bad way.' Carlo replied quickly. 'I'm just thinking that it isn't really about his wife knowing that he is dead. You want to make Servius proud, to do right by him. I understand and I'm sorry to tell you this, but I think you should hear it. He is dead. He can wait. There is no need to put yourself in danger right now to do right by someone who has passed away.'

'He isn't dead.' Carlo leaned back. Giving me a look that told me he didn't get me. And there wasn't a part of me that wanted him to understand, because I knew he never could. How could I make someone understand something I myself couldn't?

'Grieving takes time-,' Carlo started.

'I'm not grieving.' I cut him off.

'That's clear, yes. Then what is it that you are doing?' I was keeping a promise. I had made a promise to Servius that I would take his ashes and ring to his wife. That was the promise I made. A promise that I had to keep. There wasn't a time bound to it, I knew that, but the longer I waited the less of Servius was there. Moving from place to place. Moving so fast that his ghost was too busy following me. Too busy to fade into the background. Because I knew too, that sooner or later, he would.

'I'm doing what I have to do. I'm bringing his ashes and ring to his wife.' Carlo didn't answer straight away.

'You're walking into danger with open eyes?'

'So?'

'I just don't see why you would put yourself in danger for someone who isn't here anymore.'

'But he is here!' I yelled at him. My eyes were filling with tears. 'He is here! I can see him! He's here with me! Telling me what I have to do! Leading me where I have to be!.'

'And how is that going?'

'Well I found you haven't I?' Carlo didn't seem all too impressed with that. 'And now I know where he came from, Paris. I know where I have to go next. And I will follow that route. I will find my way to Paris, with or without you!.'

'You expected me to come with you?' Carlos asked in a tone that told me he thought I was going absolutely insane.

'Well, you knew Servius, didn't you?'

'I don't think I really knew him. I don't think anyone really knew him. Perhaps not even you. At least not as much as you thought. Besides, I don't owe him anything. This is not my job to handle.' there were tears streaming down my face. At any other given moment, I would have tried to hide them, but right now I couldn't. He had seen me cry, there was no point in hiding it now. He would see me as weak because I was.

'I know him, of course I know him!' Carlo looked around him, clearly uncomfortable with the situation he had created.

'I'm just trying to keep you in touch with reality.'

'Yeah, because you're in touch with reality, right? You've spent your whole life bringing Servius news when there was. I don't think you even have a life besides that. You only do things you're asked to do when you're asked!' At this point, I was full-on screaming at him. Carlo picked up his full glass of water. He had reached the point of being angry now too. He threw all the water right in my face before he walked out of the room.

CHAPTER 16

I woke up to a soft knock on my room door. The blankets stuck to my body as I stood up. My cloak was still lying at the edge of the bed. I was too tired to pick up the cloak. Not caring if people saw who I was. The mask I had had was broken and I had thrown it away.

When I opened the door a familiar figure stood in front of me. Before I could tell him to go away he forced himself through the door, into my room. He was holding a small brown leather bag. The bag clearly wasn't filled with much as it fell inwards a little bit.

'What are you doing here?' I asked Carlo.

'I'm coming with you.'

'I don't want you to come with me anymore. I can do this on my own.'

'Too bad.' Carlo said, grinning ever so slightly. He was trying to hide it, that was clear, but his eyes were filled with sorrow like I was going crazy. But I knew that there was a part of me that was going crazy. I knew that both he and I felt bad for what had happened the day before. He didn't acknowledge it, and neither did I. There was simply a silent understanding, which both of us thought was enough.

'We are leaving today.' I said.

'That's alright.' He said, raising the leather bag in the air a little like I hadn't noticed it was there.

'So no "there are dangers!" Talk anymore?'

'Oh, I'm sure you'll say that yourself when we're there.' Carlo joked. I smiled at him. Even though I had told him that I didn't want him to come along I was glad that he would. I knew that without him there would be a good chance that I would get lost along the way, ending up somewhere way further from Paris than I was now. It was good that I wouldn't be alone with Servius. That I wouldn't be able to lose myself again like I had in that pawn shop. 'So, where are we going?'

'Paris.' I answered, knowing that he of course knew that and wasn't exactly what he was asking. That we were going to Paris was clear. The truth was that I had no idea how we would actually get there.

'Yes. I was thinking we take a horse to Naples. It's not far from here, and they have a big port there. I'm sure we can find a ship there that'll take us to France. Preferably Nice. Then in Nice, we'll have to figure out how to get to Paris.' Carlo said. The thought of getting onto a horse once more wasn't one that I enjoyed all too much. Still being stiff from my travels before, but I knew that there was no other way.

'You thought this all out quite well.' I said.

'Yeah well, it was quite clear that you didn't have any plan of the sort. So I decided to think of one so that we wouldn't just go running around the place and end up somewhere worse.' Carlo said. Which was exactly what would have happened if he didn't have a plan prepared.

'That's not what I would have done.' I said despite that fact.

'I'm sure.' Carlo said, laughing. I picked up my cloak and put it on. The instant warmth felt like a hug on my skin. I checked if the ashes were still neatly tugged away and turned the ring on my finger. I put on the glove, securing the ring in place. I picked up the suitcase and mask and headed down the stairs.

The hallway and the room downstairs were empty. The sun had just risen above the horizon and there was a thin layer of mist hanging above the streets. I looked in the corner but the hooded figure wasn't there. So it must have been Carlo. There wasn't any sign of the innkeeper so I put the key on the bar and put a little coin next to it. I assumed no one would steal it and the man would be all too happy to find it lying there.

The door swung open out of Carlo's grip, caught by a gust of wind that soon found my cloak. Even though it was early, many people could be found on the street. All going on about their day. Each having their own promises to keep.

The stables were mostly empty, unlike the day that I had first arrived. The smell of the horses had reached us way before we reached the stables. One of the big doors was open and I nodded to Carlo that we should get inside. The same fat man that I had met the first day was lying on the ground. He had his back propped up against one of the stable doors and appeared to be sleeping. We exchanged a look, both of us not knowing what to do. We silently made our way over to the sleeping man. But once we stood in front of him it became clear that making as little noise as possible may not have been the best option. I looked at Carlo with a hopeful look. Carlo nodded. He began clearing his throat loudly. Which woke the man up immediately. He sprung up from where he had sat, hand hands fluttering around him like they were searching for something he could hold to protect himself. This sudden reaction made Carlo and me jump back a little. Only when the man saw my face and recognised me he began to calm down.

'Well hello there! Good to see you back! What can I do for you?' the man said, now smiling widely.

'We would like two horses please.' Carlo started.

'One.' I said to Carlo. He looked at me with a confused expression. Clearly not in the mood to share a horse. 'I have one already, it's stabled here. I'll just take him.'

'Then we would like one horse please.' Carlo corrected himself.

'That's not a problem!.' the man beamed. 'There is one in the stable right next to your horse. Now, I know you paid for two days and those haven't passed yet, but I won't give you any money back!.' the man said, looking at me. I simply nodded at him, there was no use in going against it. The fat man seemed pleased with this as he turned around walking to the stables in the back. Carlo and I followed him.

The windows in the hallway were wide open, letting the cool air get in before the heat of the day would arrive. My horse was still uncomfortably placed in the way too small stable. He moved when he saw me, but he didn't seem all too happy. I understood and felt bad for him. I shouldn't have placed him here, I should have gotten him a better spot. I was glad to take him out of it so soon already.

There was a white horse standing in the box to the right of mine. The horse had a few black spots here and there and his manes and tail were cut very short.

'This one will be yours! A real beauty it is.' the man said, signing Carlo to get closer to the horse. The horse looked a lot healthier and mine did. Though he seemed to hate the small stables just as much.

'He'll do.' Carlo said, petting the horse.

'She, it's a she!' the man said, sounding a little hurt.

'She'll do. She is indeed very beautiful.' Carlo answered quickly. The man nodded. I had to try to hold my laugh in as I saw how uncomfortable it made Carlo. I started tacking up my horse as they finished up their business.

'She'll cost you 20 lire.'

'Is her tack included?' Carlo asked.

'Yes.' Carlo gave the man three lire and began tacking up his horse as well. Now and then shooting me a glance to tell me he thought the man was absolutely insane.

* * *

Soon we found ourselves outside the stables with both our horses. The sun had risen a little higher and the heat coming from the sun was increasing with the minute. The streets had begun filling themselves with more and more people.

'We should get going.' Carlo said as he started mounting his horse. Something he did with great ease. I felt a little stupid as I followed his lead and with great difficulty raised myself into the saddle. We soon followed the dirt roads that were lain just outside of Rome.

'Where exactly is Naples?' I asked after a while when I noticed I had not a clue where we were going.

'Naples is to the south of Rome. It's a lot smaller than Rome is, but it has a big port.'

'Have you been there before?'

'No.' Carlo answered. 'But people told me about it. People who have been there. Some of the information I got back to Servius came from Naples. That's where most of the letters from France came from as well. That's why I assume we can get on a boat there that'll bring us to Nice.'

'Assume?' Carlo avoided my gaze.

'Yeah, I'm not completely sure if we can. But it seems plausible.'

'Well thought out plan indeed.' I mocked him, knowing he would throw it back to me at some point.

'Yeah, like you had a much better plan.'

We rode further while talking. Only becoming silent during the hottest hours of the day. We stopped the horses regularly near a small stream so they could drink and rest. When the evening finally came around the hotness of the day began to swell away. Filling us with renewed energy to talk.

'What's the plan for when we get there?' I asked carefully. Not knowing if he had thought out a plan or if he was still unsure what we were going to do.

'We still have some time to ponder over it. But as I see it now. Once we get there, we will sell the horses, they won't be any good on the ship. We will try and sell them for the highest price possible, hopefully, that'll give us enough to buy ourselves a trip on the boat. Then we go to the port, trying to find a ride. We will stay on the boat until we arrive at Nice. From there I guess we will have to buy new horses, if we have the money for them, and travel to Paris. Which is a long way.'

'So you have thought of a plan.'

'Of course. You still hadn't so clearly I have to be the mastermind behind all this. Carlo said. There were so many other questions I had. I knew there were many questions we shared, pondering over what their answers might be. Even questioning if we wanted to know what their answers were. If it simply would be better not to know. After last night I had begun doubting the fact that I knew Servius. Maybe I didn't know him all that well after all. There was so much information about Servius that I never even thought could be there. Maybe I didn't know him at all. Maybe I just created a version of Servius that I knew, keeping the real him from making an appearance.

'Do you think that someday you'll be able to make a plan?' Carlo asked after a long silence. I looked at him. He was facing the other way, looking at the small houses we passed. Trying to hide a smile that I could see forming on his face.

'I don't know. That might be a skill that I'll never master.'

'Clearly.' Carlo said. He looked at me, no longer hiding the enormous grin on his face.

'How come you're so good at making plans?'

'I think I have it from my mother.' he began. 'All she did was make plans. She didn't really like me or my sister very much. One of her greatest plans was to throw spaghetti in our faces when she was angry at us. Always managed to get us to shut up.'

'How was that her master plan?'

'Well, it's somewhat not fully appreciated when you throw stuff at your children. But when she was asked about it she would simply say that she was just feeding us. Kept her out of most of the trouble.'

'That explains where the stupidity of your plans come from.' Carlo laughed. When he stopped the silence returned as we continued our way towards Naples.

CHAPTER 17

When the sun had set and the cold of the evening began to make an appearance we had finally arrived at Naples. The horses were breathing heavily, tired from the journey that had taken the entire day, without any real rest. Naples was quite different from Rome. The city itself was way smaller than Rome. The houses weren't all placed together but more spread out, reaching over the mountains around it. There were many candles burning, but there were barely any lights coming out of the windows of the houses. The streets were mostly empty except for a few people who had just finished their night at the bar and were making their way home. Circling on the streets, losing their balance every few seconds. There were soldiers walking around here as well. The streets were narrow, not made for horses to walk beside each other. Carlo and I got off our horses. To my pleasure, it took Carlo just as much effort to get off the horse as me. We made our way down to a little stable that was placed close the the outer circle of the houses.

The stable was way smaller than the one in Rome had been, only reaching maybe half the size. This stable on the other hand was made out of stone, whereas the one in Rome was made out of wood. There were two big doors, one of which was wide open. Carlo and I made our way inside. Wondering if anyone would be there at this time of day. Once we entered we found a group of people sitting on the grounds. There were five boys and three girls, each with a filled glass in their hands. There either wasn't a single horse in the stable or they were all fast asleep as we couldn't hear nor see them. It didn't seem like this stable had a blooming business, Carlo seemed to notice this too.

'What are you doing here?' one of the boys asked as he jumped up. He didn't seem all too happy that we were here.

'Do you work here?' Carlo asked, equally sure about himself as the boy had been.

'Yes, but I'm not doing anything for you. Now answer my question!.'

'We were looking for a place to sell these horses.' he said turning around, pointing at both of the horses. 'But if you're not willing to do anything for us we better leave.' Carlo began to turn around as a loud voice filled the silence of the night.

'Of course, you can sell them here.' one of the other boys said as he walked towards us eagerly.

'No we can't!' the other boy argued.

'This isn't your stable!'

'Nor is it yours. What will dad say?'

'He will be glad there's finally a horse here!' the boys argued. 'For how much are you selling them?'

'40 lire per horse, saddles included.' Carlo tried, having noticed neither of these boys seemed to know a lot about business.

'20 lire per horse!' the boy argued.

'35 Lire.'

'25 Lire.' the boy said. Carlo grinned.

'Deal.' Carlo knew what he had been doing. At first, I wasn't all too sure if it would work, but it seems I was wrong. They wouldn't normally sell for 25 lire, let alone 40. The boy ran away and not long after that came back with the money. We took our belongings off the horses and handed them over to the boys, who had started their argument again and left the stable.

'Well done.' I praised Carlo as we found ourselves a few streets further. He made a large bow while walking and I couldn't help but laugh. 'So what now?'

'We go to the port.' Carlo states as if it was an obvious fact.

'Do you know where that is?' I asked Carlo.

'I assume near the water.' He replied.

Of course, he was right. After slowly making our way through the narrow streets, both walking rather uncomfortably from the long day in the saddle, we got to the port. Though what was there couldn't really be called a port. There was simply a long stretch of sand that connected to the water. There were a few wooden planks that made make-shift piers.

'What a port.' I said to Carlo. Who was just as surprised about what lay in front of us as I was.

There were three large ships placed not far from the water's edge. Though at the edge of the water, there lay some smaller boats. There were loads of people running around. The silence in which we were drowning a few streets back couldn't be found here. The voices of the shouting man echoed all around us.

'We are about to leave in a hurry!' a big man shouted who stood in the middle of the port. It was a rather odd sentence to say, but the man was so busy shouting at everyone around him that better sentences did not exit his mouth. The man was big not from fat but from muscles. His face was clearly burned, although it was difficult to see in the dark of the night. His nose was a bit crooked and he had a few golden teeth in his mouth. His eyes were stern, scanning every movement in front of him. He didn't look all too friendly.

'I think he could be able to help us.' Carlo said. He had already started walking off before I could stop him. My legs were cramping as I hurried after him. 'Hello!' Carlo said cheerfully.

'Who are you?' the man's voice was loud, as though shouting was the only level in which he spoke. It made me flinch but the man didn't seem to notice that.

'I'm Carlo, this here is Fransisco. We are looking for a ride to Nice.' The man hesitated for a little. He examined us thoroughly. His face made it seem like he was looking at a couple of ugly rats taking some of his food.

'Lucky for you she's heading to Nice.' he said as he nodded to the ship that was closest to the port. 'She leaves in half an hour. I'm feeling giving, so you might just be able to ride along. There is a price of course.'

'I wouldn't have thought otherwise. How much would it be?' said Carlo.

'If you stay on the deck four lira's, but if you want a space beneath deck, which you'll have to share it will be eight lira's. The journey will take 30 hours, we won't stop if you get sick.' the man replied. Carlo smiled kindly at the man, who didn't return the smile.

'We would like to have a space beneath the deck. Don't worry, you won't find any troubles from us.' Carlo said as the handed the money over to the man.

'Robert!' Shouted the man. Carlo nor I had expected it and jumped in the air. A thin tall man came running towards us.

'Take these two to the ship, they will stay on deck.' the man ordered, sniffing loudly. Robert nodded and waved at us to follow him. We thanked the man quickly who had already stopped paying attention to us, and followed Robert into a small rowing boat. Robert and I stepped on like it was nothing, but it took Carlo a bit more effort. His legs shook as he touched the unsteady boat on the water. Once we had all settled down Robert started rowing.

'So you will be joining us?' Robert asked excitedly.

'Yes.' Both of us answered at the same time.

'Well, welcome to the most beautiful ship you will ever see.' Robert said as we got closer to the ship. There was a robe ladder hanging from the larger ship. Which people from the smaller boats had to climb to get on board. The sails were tucking in high in the air above us. Once we got closer I had to stretch my head further and further back to be able to see the top of the ship. It was moving slowly to the rhythm of the waves. The water splashed against the side of the ship, making for a peaceful noise that rose just above the shouting that was going on all around us.

'It looks great.' I said.

'It looks better than how it feels to travel with.' Robert said as he saw the scared face of Carlo. 'But don't you worry, the trip to Nice is nice and short. So it won't be able to trouble you too much. You headed to Nice?' Robert asked. He stopped for a moment and snorted. 'Of course you're going to Nice, but are you going to stay there or are you moving along further?'

'We're headed to Paris.' I answered as Carlo seemed to have lost his voice. There was a slight shift in Robert's face. The smile that had been imprinted on his face while rowing the distance from shore to the ship had faded away. I looked around me nervously. Even though I had been on the water many times before I clasped the mask to my body, scared to drop it in the water. All of a sudden worries started to enter my brain. We had never met this man on the port, yet we fully trusted him, going on a ship that we had never seen before. Servius would never have done that. When Carlo had constructed this plan he must have thought about all the things that could go wrong, I told myself. It didn't really help, but at least I tried.

'Paris! That's cool. I wish I could travel to Paris. I used to live there but times change.'

'You're free to travel with us.' Carlo said. The words shocked me. Robert seemed nice, Carlo had noticed that too, but I simply didn't expect him to say that.

'I would love to, you two seem really nice.' he focused his words on me as he smiled widely. I smiled back and nodded back showing I thought likewise. 'But I got responsibilities and people to take care of, so the ship is where I will be.' he stopped rowing, letting the boat find its own way to the ship for the last few meters. Robert held out his left hand to stop the rowing boat from hitting the ship. He stood up and took one of the ladders that were hanging down. He nodded to us that were could climb up. I was trying to get my suitcase and mask in one hand, but that didn't work all too well.

'I'll help you carry.' Robert said as he moved his hand to the suitcase. He winked at me to say it was fine. I was glad he didn't reach for the mask and gladly handed him over the suitcase. I climbed my way up the rover ladder. It was a lot more difficult than I had expected. The wind blew the ladder to the sides. I held on to the mask more than the ladder itself. Which wasn't the best idea but after five long minutes of struggling I had found my way up to the top. One of the men on top took the mask from me, so I could lift myself over the edge. I reluctantly let go of it and quickly moved myself onto the deck. The moment I stood on both feet again I took back the mask. Hugging it to my body. It took Carlo nearly twice as long to get himself to the top. I kept looking down at him over the edge. I saw that Carlo was muttering to himself. He really didn't seem to enjoy all this. When he got near the edge I took his bag from him and helped pull him onto the deck. Rober had done this many times before and got on the ship within a minute.

'Thanks.' I told him as he handed me my suitcase back.

'Not to worry.' He moved over to Carlo. 'Well done you two. Follow me, I'll show you to your spot.' He walked away happily to the end of the ship. We walked up a few stairs when Robert opened a small door. We all had to buck to get through. Hidden behind the small door was a hallway that was home to five more small doors. He led us through the second one on the left. The room we entered was small. There were two beds on top of one another. besides that, there was one more door in the room. I wondered how many doors this ship held. When all three of us stood in the little room neither one of us could move around. 'This door leads to a hole, which you two have to share.' Robert said, squeezing his way through us with great effort. 'The captain isn't really a happy man, so you'd rather not bother him. If you have any questions feel free to ask me, I'll do my best to help you.' Robert waited for a moment. Looking at the room around him. Trying to remember if there was anything else that he had to tell us. 'Well, I think that's it. It's best to stay in here until we've started sailing away, it can get crazy up there. You'll know when that is. I will probably also check in on you once this journey, to let you know about where to get food and all. If I were you I would rest right now. Anyhow, I have to get back to work, I'll see you two later.'

'Thanks.' we both said as Robert left the room. We placed our suitcases on the floor and soon found ourselves lying on the beds, listening to the shouting that could be heard in the distance. I had placed the mask at my feet and had bound it to the bed with a piece of robe. Carlo had curiously looked at me as I did. "So it won't fall off with the swaying of the boat." I had told him. He nodded. Though the shouting could reach us it didn't take long before I dozed off.

CHAPTER 18

It had been storming on Poveglia island for longer than a week. During this week it had rained so much that the entire island lay underwater. It hadn't been all too safe to go out in this weather, especially on Poveglia. All the doctors, besides Servius and Fransisco, had been ordered to stay inside. The only people that were allowed to go out, were the nurses. It had been their job to take care of all the sick patients in Poveglia. Making it so for them that their days seemed never-ending.

Fransisco opened the door of his house. 'There you are!' Said Servius who walked over to him. Making a splashing noise with each step he took. It was still raining outside but most of the wind had settled down. Fransisco took a step outside, into the layer of water.

'Good morning to you too.' Fransisco said. The water reached him just below the knee. He closed the door behind him. 'What a weather isn't it?' He said as he pulled his cloak over his head. Servius hadn't been outside for much longer than Fransisco, but he could tell that Servius's cloak was already drenched.

'Don't start about it.' Servius grunted as he walked past Fransisco. The waves that Servius created when passing by hit Fransisco's legs, making even his knees wet.

'Thanks very much.' Fransisco muttered as he followed Servius. They slowly made their way past all the houses on the island. 'The floor in my house is completely underwater.' Fransisco said, trying to start a lighthearted conversation with Servius as he knew this day was going to be everything but lighthearted.

'I wonder why.' Servius said. Clearly not wanting any small talk.

'How many have died?' Fransisco asked Servius. They had been able to go by the hospital during this storm. Rather, they were obligated to. Having such a long storm flying over Poveglia wasn't all that pleasant. They would go to the hospital to talk to the nurses. Each one of them with bags under their eyes, shivering from the cold. Servius and Fransisco weren't able to help them all that much. They needed the doctors safe and sound and with the storm, it was impossible to get any more nurses to the island. But that wasn't the worst of all.

'34 in total, I believe. If not more have dead last night.' Servius said. Fransisco shook his head. The cold from the storm didn't help the sick people. Making them weaker and ultimately killing them. Within a weeks time 34

people had died. But with the storm all about it, had been impossible to do anything about it.

'Let's hope not.' Fransisco answered. Together walking over the the main hospital building. Poveglia had been built with the knowledge that this could happen. As each building on the island was raised, having to walk up the stairs to get in. Though the water was so high it didn't do much. Servius neared the stairs, slowing down his pace as most of the stairs were hidden beneath the water. He carefully went up the stairs step by step and Fransisco followed him. They stood together in the rain in front of the big door.

'Put on your mask' Servius said. They both secured their mask in place. Once they opened the front door a foul smell hit their nostrils. Fransisco turned around, trying to suck in some more of the fresh air before going on inside.

'Doesn't this bother you?' Fransisco asked. Servius hadn't reacted to the bad smell. Servius turned around to him. Water dripped from their cloaks onto the floor, creating a big puddle around them.

'Yes, it does. The spices and flowers in my mask are old, as are yours I suspect.' Servius answered.

'Yes, how come we don't have new ones?' Fransisco asked, shifting his mask on his face like it would help with restricting the smell.

'Everything has gone underwater. All the plants that we use for them have drowned. I assumed you knew that.' Servius said sternly. Fransisco looked at the ground, knowing that he indeed was supposed to know that. Servius turned back around and walked towards the infirmary. Fransisco followed him closely.

The smell only got worse when they entered the infirmary. Fransisco felt a little nauseous but tried his best not to let anyone notice that.

'Good morning.' Servius said. Fransisco was a little hurt that they got an actual greeting from him.

'Oh well, I don't know if it's a good morning.' One of the nurses said, walking over to them. The nurse seemed like she could collapse at any minute.

'Come sit down.' Servius said, showing her to a chair. He had noticed too that she didn't look all too good. The nurse sat down, wiping the sweat from her forehead.

'Thank you.' she said. One of the other nurses came rushing towards her, handing her a glass of water. Fransisco made it his job to gather two more chairs so he and Servius could sit too. Servius nodded to Fransisco as he gratefully took over the chair. The fact that Servius was glad to be able to sit down told Fransisco that he wasn't feeling all too good himself.

'Have any more died?' asked Servius

'Yes, two more have died last night.' the nurse said as she had finished the glass of water. 'So, a total of 36 people have died in this week.'

'Have you been able to gather them somewhere?' Servius asked. Fransisco was sure that he already knew the answer.

'No.' the nurse said softly, looking down at her lab. 'We left them in their beds.'. Neither Servius nor Fransisco was surprised by the answer. It certainly explained the foul smell that hung in the room. 'We have labeled each bed, so we know which ones are dead.'

'That's great.' Servius answered. 'It won't take all too long before we can get rid of them. My guess is that this rain will stop in two days. We should be able to burn all the bodies in a day or two after that.'

'Oh that would just be Wonderfull.' the nurse said. Fransisco couldn't have imagined how bad this had been for her. All those long days in the infirmary, constantly having to deal with this smell.

'Make sure that everything is ready, so that we can directly begin with getting them all out of here.' Servius ordered.

'I will do.' The nurse said, jumping up from her chair to join the others, letting them know their task that lies ahead. Fransisco looked at Servius, who let his gaze fly across the room. As to be guessing which one of them was dead and who was just sleeping.

'Should we help them?' Fransisco asked, feeling bad that he himself hadn't helped at all.

'No. This is not our job. We aren't any good here.' Servius said, standing up. Fransisco followed his lead. Together they walked to the front door. Stepping out of the shelter of the building back into the rain.

'So what now?' Fransisco asked, as helping wasn't an option.

'We can do nothing more but wait.' Servius answered.

CHAPTER 19

There was a soft laugh that awoke me. I didn't open my eyes. They were too heavy to lift. The bed underneath me moved in a slow rhythm, feeling so as if I was still dreaming. But I knew that I wasn't. The laughing stopped after a short while, turning into words.

'Let's just wait for him to wake up. When he does you can come out to the deck. There will be some food ready for you and we'll see if we can find you a map of France.'

'Thank you, that would be great.' another voice replied. There were footsteps moving along the floor. The sound of a creaking door reached me, a sigh, and then silence. After a while I found the energy to open my eyes. There was almost no light coming into the room. Except from the gaps in the wall, that let in just enough light to be able to see the room around me. The mask was hanging from the bed slightly, but the robe was still bound to it. The suitcase lay on the same spot on the ground, despite all the movements of the ship. That's where I was. That's where all the motions came from. My mouth was dry and my entire body was aching from the long day of horse riding before. I wasn't looking forward to when we would reach land again. I knew that would mean an even longer horse ride. I didn't know if my body could manage that. I wasn't all too sure how long it would take us from Nice to Paris, but I knew that however long it was, it would be way too long. But that was something that I would worry about later.

'Are you awake?' A voice said that belonged to the head that was now towering over me, looking me in my eyes. I mumbled an answer that even I couldn't really understand. I moved my body, hoping that the movement would wake me up. The pain that shot through my legs did in fact wake me up. I grunted. Carlo laughed at me. He didn't seem all too stiff from the day before. Easily moving himself around the small room. 'I think you're awake. Are your legs hurting? I can feel a little something in mine too, but it isn't too bad. I had just talked to Robert. We can go and get some food once you get out of bed. He was telling me that they use francs in France, instead of Lire. We can change some of our money with him. We can still use Lire in Paris if we want to. We will talk about that later. Oh, and I managed to get us a map. That'll definitely help us.' Carlo said cheerfully. I only took in about half of what he said, as I raised myself into a sitting position on the edge of my bed.

'And you made a new friend I heard.' I mocked him.

'I wish, he would make great company. Way better than you do.' he replied, sitting down next to me.

'Thanks.' I said. We both laughed. I had no idea how we had become so close to one another in such a short time. But we had. And so had he with Robert. Becoming close to someone had always seemed like a difficult task with me. It always seemed hard or even impossible. It surely wasn't easy with Servius. But it seemed that not everyone had such a hard shell as Servius had had. Talking to someone and being friends are two different things. There is so much more to being friends than just talking. There are things that are expected from you. Thing that wouldn't ever be said out loud, but that you just had to know. The things that were expected from me with Carlo were vastly different from those that were expected from me with Servius.

'Let's get dressed and see what is going on outside.' Carlo said, interrupting my thoughts.

'Sure.' I answered. Though it took me a good while before I got up. My legs weren't functioning making it almost impossible to keep balance despite the movements of the ship.

When we opened the door to the deck my eyes squinted. The light of the rising sun was so bright it made my eyes water. There were many people outside and the shouting had not settled down any. Shouting that I hadn't noticed when I first woke up. Apparently I had gotten used to it in the little time that we had spent on the boat. Blinded and deafened by the world around me we made our way down the deck. When I looked around the horizon, the only thing that I could see was the water that surrounded us. The waves splashed against the side of the ship. The sails were down, catching the wind with great measures, making the ships go at an incredibly fast pace. The deck itself was filled with a thin layer of water. It must have rained while we were asleep, though the layer of mist that often accompanied night rain was nowhere to be found.

'Well, good morning to you!.' Robert said as he approached us. His words were pointed towards me.

'Morning.' I replied. His figure was taller than it had seemed the night before. His hair was black and he had a small beard. His eyes were brown and kindly set. His face was slightly burned from the many hours he spent in the sun. He had a big smile on his face that made it difficult not to smile back.

'I didn't think you would wake up.' he said jokingly. All I did was give him a short laugh as I stared out at the sea. 'Not much of a talker?' he asked. I had never been much of a talker. There weren't many people on Poveglia that I could talk to and so I had learned to make myself quiet company. I hoped that Robert didn't need an answer from me, but his hopeful eyes kept looking at me. It made me a bit worried. Carlo seemed to really like Robert. I was scared that if I started to talk, letting him get to know the plague doctor in front of him, I would scare him away. I didn't want to ruin the possible friendship between Carlo and him.

'No, not much. I tend to scare people off once I start to talk.' I said, looking from Carlo to Robert. They were both looking at me.

'Scare me off? Good luck with that. I'm not one to get scared off easily. Why would you scare me off?' Robert asked.

'I'm a plague doctor.' I said awkwardly. I realised that I did not have the mask with me. Maybe if I hadn't said it he wouldn't have noticed. Maybe I had ruined it without meaning to.

'And I'm a sailor.' Robert said. I looked at him with confusion. 'We are both terrifying to different people. You are terrifying to people whose egos are greater than their brains. I am terrifying to people who are scared of boats and get seasick.' I laughed out loud. Knowing that he didn't really have a point, but being grateful that he tried to make me feel better.

'I guess you're right.' I said.

'You two seem to be becoming friends.' Carlo said. I knew what he was getting at. Robert smiled at this remark as though he had never been called a friend before. I was sure that I was smiling in the same way.

'Not as good as you two are.' I answered, which made Carlo join the smiling. I was sure that to everyone around us, we looked like complete idiots.

'I spoke with the captain, he is able to change the money for you. For a small price, of course, you know how they are. But if you do that he will give you the map for free. Do you want that?' Robert said. He looked at me first and I nodded. Then his gaze went over to Carlo and he nodded as well.

We followed Robert as he walked to the back of the ship. There were two stairs on each side of the ship. It was a hell getting on the top of them. Each step I took I thought would be my last one, holding on tight to the railing to keep myself from losing my balance. The captain was standing behind the wheel of the ship. The wheel was bound tight to the ship by a robe, making sure that the boat wouldn't sail somewhere it wasn't supposed to.

'There you are!.' the captain shouted at Robert.

'Sorry. It took a little longer than expected.' he moved to the side so that the captain could look at us clearly. 'They're willing to change their money with you.' he said.

'Good. Let's get somewhere private. And you-,' he said to Robert. 'get back to work!' Robert nodded and went off. The captain took us down the stairs again. My legs were screaming and in my head, I was cursing him for it. We entered the same door we had to enter to get to our room. Though this time were entered the door at the end of the hallway. The door creaked just like ours had. It seemed to be a reoccurring habit these doors had. The room inside was about twelve times the size of our little room. The room was decorated with tables, a large wooden desk, chairs, and multiple wardrobes. There were even a few paintings hanging on the walls.

'Take a seat.' the captain ordered after he had sat himself down on the large chair that stood behind the desk. The chairs were small and round, making it awkward to sit in if you were larger than the chair itself. The movement of the boat made me grasp the edge of the chair, hoping I wouldn't fall out of it; even though that was practically impossible. 'You wanted to trade lire to francs?' the captain said, as though he wasn't sure of that fact at all.

'Yes.' I answered. Carlo looked around him nervously.

'Great, great. I am just the guy for that.' his hand went down to one of the drawers of the desk. He opened it showing a rather large bag that I assumed was filled with coins. He opened the bag, spreading some of the coins out on the table. 'These coins here are francs.' he said proudly. 'How many lire do you have?' Carlo looked at me uncertainly.

'I have 20.' Carlo whispered to me.

'I think I have about 85 left.' I whispered back. I didn't speak too softly, and the captain cried out as he heard.

'You?! 85 lire?! You must be kidding!' the captain began. 'Where did you get that money? You're only a miserable little doctor! Did you steal it from the people who died by your hands?!' the captain spit out.

'We would like to change 90 lire.' Carlo said. Ignoring the remarks of the captain. I was glad Carlo changed the subject as I wasn't sure I would have been able to. It was bothering me what the captain had said. Why would I steal from people who died?

'Very well.' the captain said. Gathering together a load of coins. 'With that many Lire, I can give you 40 francs. I won't give you more, so don't try.'

'We were told that you would give us a map with that as well.' Carlo said as I handed him some of my lire.

'That'll cost you money.' the captain tried. I would have probably accepted it, but Carlo certainly didn't.

'No, I don't think so. We were told that you would give it to us for free if we exchanged our money with you. So we will be getting it for free.' said Carlo, sounding very sure of himself.

'Very well.' said the captain, sounding impressed. Carlo handed him over the 90 lire. The captain took them and counted them carefully. When he was sure we had given him the right amount of money he handed us the 40 francs. He opened another drawer and handed us the map. He gave us what we wanted, so we ended it there. We thanked the captain and stood up to leave. 'Robert Will be down here. The first door to the left. I'm sure he will be able to tell you how to get to Paris.' the captain said as we left the room.

We entered the door on the left which revealed a small staircase down. It wasn't visible where the stairs led but the stairs themselves didn't seem all too sturdy.

'You first.' I said. Carlo reluctantly found his way down the stairs. Not having the mask in my hand came in quite handy when walking down the stairs. Walking down such narrow steps was difficult in and of itself, let alone with the movement of the ship, bouncing you from wall to wall. When we got down there was another door, that when opened, showed a big room. There were long wooden tables at which the crew of the ship sat and ate while talking and signing loudly. Carlo nodded towards a sort of kitchen where people filled their plates with food. Robert stood in the line, taking food on his plate. More than you would have expected by how rather thin he was. When he was done he turned around. The moment he locked eyes with us he began to wave enthusiastically for us to come over.

'How did it go?' he asked as we got close enough to him to start a conversation. He didn't have Carlo or me enough time to answer as he kept talking. 'Take some food, then we'll sit down and talk.' Carlo didn't need to hear that for a second time. He picked up a plate and began to fill it. I reluctantly did the same. There wasn't a part of me that wanted to eat. I hadn't eaten much since Servius. I told myself that I had been too busy to eat. Together with the fact that this food didn't look all that appetising, I filled my plate rather scarcely.

Once we had both filled our plates we bade our way back to Robert. They both shot a quick glance at my plate. I saw this but didn't look them in the eyes to prevent them from saying anything about it.

The sound of our footsteps was overshadowed by the loud singing that had started once more. We took place at a table near the end, leaving much room between us and the others; who didn't seem too happy by our appearance. Thought neither did they with the appearance of Robert, which I hadn't expected. 'So, how did it go?' Robert asked once more.

'Great, we got the francs and the map. He didn't want to give us the map for free at first, but we got him to do it in the end.' Carlo answered. I was glad Carlo answered, as I did not want to do it.

'Nicely done. Not many people dare go against him.' Robert said, taking a heap of food from his plate and putting it in his mouth.

'It makes it easier that I don't know him. I wouldn't know what to be scared of.' Carlo said bravely. We all ate in silence for a while.

'Hi, Robert.' one of the sailors said as he walked by. Robert raised his hand in reply but didn't say anything. This was the first time I had seen any one of the sailors talk to Robert.

Many of the men had left by the time that we were done eating. The sudden silence made the plashing of the waves against the ship loud. We put our plates together and Carlo stood up to bring them back. His body staggered while walking, trying to keep his balance as the ship swayed more than it had before. A small laugh escaped Robert's mouth.

'The captain told us you can show us the route to Paris.' I said.

'I am not sure if I know the best route, but I can give you one, yes. Show me the map.' Robert replied. I got the map out of the pocket of my cloak and folded it open. I put it down on the table as Robert went to get a pen. The map was big, taking up most of the table. It was a map of only France, with the names of most of the cities and villages on it. Nice was a place down on the south while Paris lay more on the northern side of France. Seeing the distance on this map made me realise just how long our journey would be. Some part of me wanted to stop. To just go back to Poveglia. To get my stuff back on the island, to spend the rest of my days there. But I couldn't. I had made a promise. Robert picked up his pen and put a circle around Nice and Paris. The map was made out of multiple shades of brown. The darker the brown the higher the mountain. There was a big mountain between the two places, which we would probably have to cross.

'Okay.' said Robert, as Carlo sat back down, holding the table for stability. 'This mountain here could be a small problem. You could go over it, or you could find a way around it. If you go sort of straight both it will take you about ten days. If you go around the mountain it can take you up to 16 days.'

'I think it will be better to go over the mountains.' I began. 'We can see if there are any inns in the mountain where we could stay the night and perhaps trade the horses. So we know for sure they can bring us to Paris.'

'Sounds like a plan.' Carlo said, giving me a wink. I shook my head in response.

'That sounds good.' Robert said, beginning to draw a line on the map. His pen made a scratching noise as he moved it along. Following a small line that connected to multiple larger ones. The line was almost completely straight if you looked at it in its completion. I hoped that it would make it easier for us to find our way. 'I think this is the best route to take. I don't think you will find many inns in the mountains. So you'll be sleeping under the stars for most of it. But there might perhaps be one where you can switch horses.' Robert said as he drew the last centimeter to Paris. He held up his pen, looking proudly at the line he had drawn. Both Carlo and I studied the line for a while.

'Thank you.' I said after a long pause.

'No problem.' Robert answered. He was smiling though his eyes were filled with sadness. The people on the ship didn't seem to talk to him much. Maybe he was sad that we were about to leave. Maybe that's why the captain put him up with us. Or perhaps it was because the captain didn't like him and thought this would be extra trouble for him.

'Ten days, right?' Carlo asked.

'Yes, if you keep going.' Robert answered. Carlo nodded.

'That will be a hell of a ride.' I said.

'Are you going to stay in France?' Robert asked in a low voice.

'That's not the plan I have.' Carlo said quickly.

'Mine neither. I think we just get it done and then we'll go back to Rome. And I'll go back to Venice I guess.' Robert seemed to be enlightened by that.

'Oh, you're on a mission?' Robert asked.

'Sort of.' I answered. Robert looked at me hopefully but I didn't explain it further.

'Let's go to the deck, I think we will be there soon.' Robert said, walking away. I quickly folded the map back up and followed him out.

It was clear that when we had gotten out this morning, part of the crew wasn't out and about. The deck of the ship was overflowing with people running around, changing the direction of the sails, making sure the ship was sailing towards land. We went out to the front of the ship, looking in front of us until a stroke of land became visible.

'Land!' One of the men shouted. The sound was echoed all the way down to the back of the ship. The ship was going at an incredible speed as a lot of things started happening around me. There were men running around, loosening the sails, clearing up space, and doing other things I did not know about. The captain took his spot behind the wheel.

'You better get your stuff packed' Robert said before he ran off to help the others.

CHAPTER 20

The shouting could be heard from the little room we shared. We were done packing within a minute but decided to stay in the room a little longer. We didn't want to be a bother to whatever was going on outside.

'We could have told him.' Carlo said. He stood leaning against the wall opposite the bed I was sitting on.

'We could have told Whom what?' I asked, not sure of what he meant.

'Robert. We could have told him what we would be doing in Paris.'

'Why should we have told him? There is no use in him knowing.'

'It would have been nice too.' Carlo snarled.

'Why?'

'He's rather lonely, don't you see?'

'So telling him about all the great adventures that he will be missing out on is nice for him?' I said. Carlo thought about this for a moment. 'I can tell he is lonely too. And I wish he could come along, he seems really nice. But I don't think it's an option for him.'

'I know.' Carlo said. I waited for him to say something more, but he didn't.

The shouting outside slowly turned into chanting. The boat had begun to slow down and after a few more hours it had stopped completely. Carlo, who had been studying the map, folded it back up and put it in his pocket. We waited just a little longer before going out of our room.

'Should we go check it out?' Carlo said and I nodded. We slowly made our way out of the room and onto the deck. Giving space to all the men running around on the ship. Most of the men were already on land, though that didn't make it any less of a chaos on the ship. Robert was standing at the edge of the ship looking over the land.

'Hello.' I said, leaning against the ship beside him.

'Hello.' He replied dully. Carlo didn't say anything but kept close.

'So, we're here.' I said. I couldn't wait to get off the ship and find some peace down below.

'Yes, we are.' Robert replied dully. He did not take his gaze away from the city. It was the middle of the day. There were many people out and about in the city. None of them looked up at the big ship we were on. The houses were completely different from those in Rome and Venice. Though I couldn't quite explain why that was. Maybe it was the colour of the houses that were rather yellow or the more decorations on them. With bigger streets in between them and less water taking over the city. 'It won't be long before you two can go down.' Robert said.

'That's great.' I replied. Giving a quick glance at Carlo, hoping for some help, but Carlo didn't know what to make of it either.

'Yeah.' Robert answered. He tried to smile but it wasn't convincing.

'Will you be okay?' Carlo asked.

'Shouldn't I ask you that? Not to be rude but, you're about to go on a journey with clearly no idea how to use a map.' Robert said, mainly looking at me. That hurt a little.

'I do know how to use a map!' I said. Robert didn't seem to believe me.

'Okay okay.' He said as we both smiled, looking at the view in front of us. 'About what you said. That you were worried to scare me away. I don't know why you believe that, but it must have a good reason. I know I sound like a bit of a cliché saying this but don't worry about what people think of you. Because no matter how hard you try, if they want to see you a certain way, they will. There's nothing to do about that. It's a shame to ponder over something you can't change. I know that it isn't all that easy, but one day you'll acquire that skill.' Robert said. We stood in silence for a moment. The world around us seemed to have disappeared for a moment.

'Do you have that skill?' I asked him.

'Not yet.' He replied. He waited a moment before continuing, looking down at the people on the port. He raised his head, looking me in the eyes. 'But I hope that soon enough I will.'

'I hope you will.' I said. He smiled kindly. It hurt me to let him hear like this. He was really kind and had helped us a lot. There was a part of me that wanted him to come along. The three of us going to Paris. But I knew that he couldn't. Robert cleared his throat.

'My real name isn't Robert.' He said. I looked at him surprised. I wasn't all too sure what to make of it.

'Then what is it?' Carlo asked, eagerly wanting to know who Robert really was.

'Samuele.'

'Samuele?' Carlo and I said in chorus.

'Yes, it sucks. You don't know how many times I've been told that I am the devil. That's why I chose to change it. To tell everyone my name is Robert. No more annoying Catholics this way.' Robert smiled. I smiled back at him. I understood a little of his troubles. Though it wasn't the same of course, I could imagine what he would have felt like.

'Well, thank you, Samuele.' I said. Robert gave me a sincere smile back. He still didn't seem all too happy that we were leaving.

'It's time to get you on land.' Robert said. I bound the mask to my leg so that I had two hands to climb down the robe. It hit the side of the boat with each step I took, but it didn't fall down and the mask was still in one piece when my feet hit the ground. It took Carlo a greater deal of effort to get down, swinging around on the robe, inching himself down. When we were both on the ground we looked up at Robert. We waited a moment but he didn't move. Robert waived at us from up on the boat. Carlo and I both reluctantly waived back. Neither one of us wanted to let him go. I could tell that Carlo really hoped that Robert would have changed his mind and come along. secretly I had hoped that too. We stood there for a while. Robert was the one to walk away first. We made friends with our goodbye and turned around to take in the city.

CHAPTER 21

We walked on the port, going over to where the ships met the houses. There were many houses stalled away around the port, even going uphill a bit. The houses never reached the top of the hill, making the hill seem taller than it actually was.

All the streets were bigger than they had been in Italy. The sea kept a good distance from the city and there were mountains all around us visible on the horizon. When we looked to the left of us we saw a big hill at the end of the street. On it stood what could have been the remains of a castle.

'That hill.' Carlo said as he pointed at the same hill that I had been looking at. 'There used to be a castle on there. But it was destroyed when Louis the 14th came to rule.'

'Why did he destroy it?' I asked, surprised that Carlo knew this.

'No idea.' He answered as he raised his shoulders.

'How do you know about that hill anyways?' I said as we walked towards it to get a better look.

'Someone who had traveled here told me about it. It apparently stuck with me.' Carlo stopped walking for a moment. Letting the sun hit his face before he spoke once more. 'We do have one problem.' he said. 'I do not speak French.' he looked at me with what I assumed was guilt.

'Not to worry, I do speak French.' I answered.

'You do?' Carlo said. He actually looked very surprised by this. Something I hadn't expected him to be.

'Yes. Servius taught me.' I said.

'Ah, of course! That's explains it.' Carlo said as we started to walk once more. We didn't continue on to the ruins but instead walked around a bit, trying to find a stable.

'Were all the letters he got in French?' I asked Carlo.

'I don't know. I didn't open them all that much. I only got a look at the ones that were already open when I got them. But all those were written in French, yes.' Carlo answered. I nodded my head at this. There were as many people in Nice as there had been in Rome. It was rather odd to see that it was so busy everywhere. I didn't know what I thought of it, but I wasn't all that fond of it.

We followed a long beach for a while. Both still a little unsteady on our feet from the boat ride. The sea was moving peacefully in the distance. The beach was rather empty compared to the city, even though the temperature had begun to rise.

'Do you have any idea where we have to go?' I asked Carlo after a while. I already knew the answer.

'Nope.' he simply replied.

'Okay.' I said and so we walked. We had walked for most of the day when we came across a big bridge at the end of the city. The bridge was incredibly wide but not at all long. There was a river running underneath it. The bridge was occupied by many carriages being pulled forward by horses. We walked close to the side of the bridge, out of the way from other people who were trying to pass. I grabbed the railing at one point when a carriage passed us at a rather narrow distance. I was sure that I wouldn't fall in, but grabbing hold of it gave me a sense of security.

After we had crossed the bridge it hadn't taken us long before we found a stable. The stable wasn't all too big, but the space around it was. There were endless green fields filled with more horses than I could count. We walked in and were happily greeted. We asked for two horses and without much delay we were guided outside. We stood near one of the fences as the guys who were helping us made their way over the big field to get us two horses. The third guy stayed at the fence with us.

'How much will they be?' I asked as I saw the two guys come back. Both of them lead an appaloosa. Both horses were black and white and they almost seemed to be the same horse.

'Twenty francs.' the guy said.

'Is tack included?' I asked

'Yes.' the man replied. Neither Carlo nor I knew if that was much or not, so we gave him the money. The two guys took them inside while we waited for them to tack the horses up. The evening sun made for a pleasant temperature. Not much later the guys got back out, handing us over the horses. We thanked them and walked off. The horses' saddles came with saddlebags. I tried to put the plague mask in one of them, but it was a little bit too big. I secured the half that stuck out of it with a piece of robe. I tied the suitcase to the other end of the saddle. We walked away a bit from the city before getting on. We walked until the sun began to set.

'Let's stop and eat first.' Carlo said. Before we had crossed the bridge we had stopped at a small shop that sold food and had gotten enough to last us for most of the trip. At least until we hoped to find an inn. We stopped by the side of the road. There weren't many people about anymore, and where we stood seemed to be a no man's land. We bound the horses to a tree and sat down in the grass.

'I think we will have to ride in the dark today.' I said. There was always an option to not ride in the dark, but I wanted to make kilometers quickly.

'I agree.' Carlo said. I was glad he did. We quickly ate some of the food as we watched the sunset. We didn't speak that much during our meal. It felt as though we had gone through everything there was to say. I didn't mind it, though it worried me to think that it bothered Carlo.

When we had finished eating we packed all our stuff to continue. I took out the glass bottle from my cloak. The bottle had warmed up from my body heat. The ash had begun to fasten itself to the bottle a little. There was damp inside the bottle, but I didn't dare let it out. Scared that I would accidentally lose a part of Servius. I gave the bottle a little tap before I put it back in my cloak.

We mounted on the horses and rode further in the dark. The horses that we got were better than the ones we had when we traveled from Rome to Naples. These horses were fed well and held energy. They had muscles. It felt like they were actually able to bring us over the big mountains. This gave me some newfound hope that the route to Paris maybe wouldn't just be all hell. Something that I would probably not agree with a few days later.

CHAPTER 22

It had been easy going on Poveglia for over a month now. Stuck in the same old dull routine. Wake up, go to the infirmary, check the deaths, make sure people were burned, eat dinner, and sleep. Fransisco had noticed that Servius had gotten sick of it too. Often telling Fransisco that he had other work to do, leaving him to fend for himself. Fransisco hadn't complained and done as he was asked. After all, it had seemed like Servius had been busy planning something. Suddenly making a lot of trips to Venice. Fransisco hadn't dared to ask what he was doing as times had taught him that he would eventually know.

'Fransisco!' Servius shouted. Francisco had been walking from his house to the infirmary when he heard the voice. He stopped dead in his tracks, turning around to see Servius standing near the housing. He waived at Fransisco to go to him. Fransisco didn't wait and went to see what Servius wanted from him. 'Come over here.' Servius said as Fransisco got near.

They together walked around the corner of the housing. Fransisco had thought that Servius would take him to his house but Fransisco had been wrong. Servius kept walking to the edge of the island. There they found a small boat filled with boxes and an old man standing on the edge.

'Good morning!.' The man said to Fransisco. Fransisco greeted him back.

'Help me with these.' Servius said as he jumped in the little boat, handing over the boxes to Fransisco. Together they got all the boxes on land and brought them over to a little table that stood against the side of the infirmary. Fransisco hadn't been sure if it was the beautiful weather or the fear of what was inside that had made the man want to work outside. The sky was clear and only the tops of the trees were slightly moving in the wind.

'Who is he?' Fransisco whispered to Servius. He had been certain that the man hadn't heard him, which was what surprised him when the man started to answer.

'My name is Eugenio!' the old man beamed out proudly. 'I am the world's greatest mask maker.'

'A mask maker?' Fransisco asked. Servius gave Fransisco a look that told him it was rather obvious.

'Yes. You hold that thing in your arms there.' the man said, pointing at the mask that Fransisco was holding in his hands. 'I make them. A lot better than that one. You desperately need a new one.' the man said.

'He sure does. This one stinks.' Servius said, looking at Fransisco while smiling widely.

The man stalled out all his equipment and started to work. He took some measurements of Fransisco's face and took the old mask from his as a reference. Without a mask, Fransisco couldn't do much on the island. It would be too dangerous for him to go into the infirmary. So Fransisco spends his day sitting by the water, letting the sun hit his face. Enjoying a day filled with nothing. A day finally different from all the others.

'May I join you?' Servius asked. Fransisco nodded to him and Servius sat down next to him. 'He took my measurements too. There is nothing to do now but wait.' Servius said, looking at Fransisco. 'But you already figured that out I see.'. Fransisco looked at Servius for a moment. He had his eyes closed and seemed to be enjoying a bit of peace.

'It's nice to finally do something different.' Fransisco started. Servius opened his eyes.

'Are you getting bored?' Servius asked. Fransisco hoped that he was joking but he knew different.

'No. Perhaps. Maybe a bit.' Fransisco started. 'It just gets redundant doing the same thing over and over again. Day after day. Sometimes it feels like I'm not even alive. That I am like a zombie. Walking over the island, doing my tasks without really being there.' Fransisco looked hopeful at Servius.

'I know what you mean.' Servius replied. 'I felt like that a long time too. Maybe I still do a little. I know you think that it may not be the same because I am not here all the time. But that doesn't matter.' Servius touched the water with the tip of his shoe.

'Doesn't it?' Fransisco asked. To him, it would make a great deal of difference. He would give anything to get off the island for a day. To do something different, to get a different view.

'No, it doesn't.' Servius said gloomy. 'No matter how hard you try, no matter how different each day looks. The people on the island will die. And there is nothing that we can do about it.'.

CHAPTER 23

The first two days on the road were fine. The roads themselves were great and there wasn't any sort of resistance. The weather wasn't too hot or too cold. We made many kilometers, following the line on the map narrowly. The days were utterly boring as nothing exited happened.

The road that we had just turned on was a long one. We would have to follow it for at least a few hours. We decided that we would ride this one out and at the end of it give the horses and ourselves some well-deserved rest. It had stayed silent between the two of us for a while, but that couldn't last.

'It's sad that Robert couldn't join us.' Carlo began. He had stated that thought many times over the past two days. I was getting a little annoyed that Carlo kept bringing it up.

'I know. You've told me that many times already. But he had his reasons not to join us.' I stopped for a moment. Weighing whether or not to say what I was thinking. I did. 'It could have been dangerous to take him.' I said. Carlo stopped his horse. Looking at me with disbelief.

'Dangerous?' Carlo gasped. He didn't sound all too happy about that word, but I had a feeling he knew what I was talking about.

'We are here to get Servius's ash and ring to his wife. I have a task to do. I trust you. Maybe I shouldn't have, but so far you've given me no reason not to. Servius trusted you. So I do too. That wasn't a decision that I made, he did that for me. And I trust Servius to make the right decision. But we do not know if we could trust Robert. He didn't know Servius.' I said. Carlo got his horse back to a slow walk.

'We don't know if he doesn't know Servius. We never asked him.' Carlo replied.

'I know, but let's be honest. What are the odds that he would have known Servius?' I slowed down my horse so that we would be riding next to each other once more.

'I understand. And perhaps you have a point. Maybe he wasn't to trust, though I highly doubt it. I just didn't want to leave him behind. He looked...' Carlo didn't finish his sentence.

'Sad?' I offered. Carlo nodded.

'When we have finished what we started and go back. Perhaps we can do something more. Maybe he can come along with us. Or perhaps we would just keep in touch with him. But first Servius. There is no use in pondering over that matter now.' I said. And that was it. Carlo didn't answer. I couldn't quite tell if he was angry with me or not. I knew that he didn't care all that much about Servius like I do. Maybe he thought I was obsessed with doing this thing for Servius. Maybe he was right, maybe I was. I don't know when an obsession starts to be an obsession. Maybe I had passed that line a long time ago. I liked to believe that that line was still a good way in front of me.

We had spent a total of four days on the road when we actually reached the mountains. We had already been going uphill for quite some time, but the actual climb just started now. It took us hours to get further up the mountain, making very little kilometers. Letting the horses rest every few hours. We didn't know how much climbing they could take at a time but thought that a few hours would be alright. The forest around us had gotten dense. There were different sounds escaping from behind every tree. Birds, squirrels, and maybe even larger animals kept us company throughout the day. The horses didn't seem all too bothered by them. We didn't meet many people on this route. Not that we thought that was odd. It was a daring road to take, especially with horses. The road often became very narrow, almost too narrow for one horse to walk. There were often loose stones at these parts and our horses had almost tripped many times. But we didn't know if there was another route we could take, so we followed the one that was drawn out for us.

Many hours later we made our way up the last few meters of the mountain. Both the horses and we were panting. They had been slowing down the last couple hundred meters. My legs were burning from the day's ride and I could only pity the horses. Their work had been way harder than ours. Dragging us all the way up the mountain. Their legs must be hurting too. Both Carlo and I decided to walk next to our horses once the climbing had stopped. The horses seemed the be grateful for it as their tempo began to increase again. We hoped that this would prevent the horses from overworking. Neither of us was really good with horses, so maybe it had already been too late. When we reached the top there was a plain stretched out piece of land in front of us. after walking over it for a while a wooden inn came into our view.

The inn was placed off to the side, standing in the middle of the woods. The empty piece of land on the other side of the road had been turned into a fenced field, that was occupied by two horses. I looked over at Carlo, whose face had lit up. We both couldn't be happier to see this inn. We had been looking out for it since we started the climb. The longer it took us the less hope we got that it actually existed. We hurried over to the inn. There weren't any people about, and taking a quick glance through the window told me that there was no one inside either. I wasn't too worried about it. The horses that stood outside seemed to be in great condition. That meant that someone was here taking care of them. We stood in front of the door. Carlo handed his horse over to me.

'I'll go inside to ask if they have a place for us.' Carlo said.

'Sounds good. How long do you think we will stay here?' I asked.

'Just one day, I reckon.' Carlo said as he walked through the door on inside.

'Yeah, good.' I said, not sure if Carlo heard me. I didn't want to stay here any longer than needed. I was glad Carlo thought the same. If he had wanted to stay longer I wouldn't have argued with him though. He was traveling with me, sure, but that didn't mean that I should make it a living hell for him. A loud chirping bird flew over, making the horses look up. They dragged my arm up and made me turn around. I was now facing the field. The two horses that stood out in the field were big work horses, both brown with black manes. The fence that surrounded the field was broken in many places. Despite the broken wood, the horses stayed where they were. I could only hope that our horses would do the same.

I stood there for a long time. Looking at the wonderful nature around me. Wondering what took Carlo so long. It came to me then that Carlo had said he didn't speak French. I wondered if that was the reason he hadn't come out yet. But I let that thought go quickly. If Carlo noticed they didn't speak Italian he would have come outside to send me in. As I thought that, I heard an upbeat voice behind me.

'They have a room for us!.' Carlo beamed. I turned around to see Carlo walk out of the inn. 'We can stay here for the night. We share a room. The horses can stay with the other two and they will get food. And it all comes down to five francs!' Carlo said proudly, swinging his arms up in the air. 'I don't actually know if that is a lot or not, but it doesn't sound too expensive. Oh, and we get dinner!.' he added.

'Sound good.' I beamed as I handed him back his horse. We turned the horses around and walked to the field. It didn't take long before we had gotten all the tack off and the horses were running around freely. Not that they ran for long. It took less than ten seconds before they abruptly stopped and began eating the grass underneath their feet. We made sure the horses looked happy before picking up our stuff and walking towards the inn.

The inside of the inn smelled like food that had been burned. It wasn't the worst smell I had ever smelled, but it wasn't all too pleasant. We were greeted by an old lady who showed us our room. Though we were exhausted from the ride our empty bellies screamed louder. We quickly washed up, trying to get rid of most of the sweat that had formed on our body like a second layer of skin. When we were done we quickly went back down to eat.

The table was set out for us. It was a small round wooden table, with two chairs standing at its side. On the table stood two plates and glasses ready for us to use. We made our way to the table, looking around us if anyone was there but they weren't. We sat down, hoping that this table was indeed made for us. We didn't have to wait long for that answer. As soon as we made ourselves comfortable the old lady came back into the room.

'I've made stew for today, so that is what you two will get.' she said in a stern voice, but with a big smile on her face.

'Thank you.' we both answered quickly as she filled our glasses with water. I chugged mine down in one go before the lady had even time to leave. When I put back down my glass I saw that Carlo had done the same thing. She saw this and waited. Filling our glasses once more before she left again, all while laughing at us. We had both finished our second glass when the lady came back carrying a small pot of stew. She lifted the pot above the table and placed it in the middle of us. We mumbled thanks as we greedily began to fill our plates. Pouring a big spoon of stew on my plate the smell hit my nose. My mouth began to water even more than it had had before. I took the first bite but was punished for being too greedy. The hot stew burned my mouth. I spit out the stew by surprise and began to blow on it. Carlo had seen what happened to me and didn't make the same mistake. The lady came back once more with freshly baked bread. We thanked her once more when accepting the bread. We didn't start talking before we had finished our first plate.

'How is the food gentlemen?' a small set man asked as we had finished both the stew and the bread.

'It was truly amazing.' Carlo answered.

'The best stew I have ever had.' I added.

'Well that is great!.' the man said. He turned around. I followed his gaze and saw that the old lady sat at a table in the other corner of the room. I hadn't noticed her sit down. The lady smiled widely and giggled to herself. 'How about a glass of wine? It's on the house.' the small man asked. Carlo and I exchanged a quick look and we both nodded.

'Why not?' I answered. I had never drunk any wine. It wasn't something we drank on Poveglia. The only thing we drank on Poveglia was stale water and an occasional beer. This looked more enjoyable than both had been. I was slightly shocked that the man filled our glasses to the brim. I could hardly pick it up without spilling anything.

'So you two are from Italy. But from where in Italy?' the man asked. I was slightly taken aback by the fact that he knew we were from Italy. But that didn't take all too long. I quickly realised that he had been talking in Italian to us.

'We are from Rome.' Carlo answered quickly. I didn't quite understand why, but it seemed like he wasn't too keen on telling the man where I was from. Maybe I had gotten him to worry about trust a little too much.

'Rome! Very well! You've come from a beautiful city. What makes you come here?' the man continued asking. Having already drunk most of his glass of wine. I myself had only taken a few sips. The wine tasted vastly different from what I had expected, but I liked it nonetheless.

'We're on our way to Paris.' Carlo answered.

'Oh, very well! You want to see Napoleon?' the man laughed, though his question seemed sincere. I looked up at that, suddenly a lot more interested in where the conversation was going. Jean and Pierre weren't all that fond of Napoleon and I was curious if it was the same for others as well.

'Is he in Paris?' Carlo asked, after seeing the expression on my face.

'Oh, no. He is not. But the people who love him are. And the people who hate him. He himself is on the battlefield. The bravery of the man is quite amazing.' the man said, gulping the rest of his wine.

'I have come to notice that there are a lot of people who aren't so fond of him.' I spoke out carefully. Scared to make the man in front of me angry. The man snorted before he began to speak.

'Those people don't know what they are talking about. They are just cowards, too scared to fight for what is right. Many of them have married just so they wouldn't need to go to the battlefield. As I said, cowards. No, no, no, Napoleon is a good guy. The man before him wasn't. Those people just aren't used to a true leader.' the man said. Pouring himself another drink.

'Who reigned before him?' I asked, leaning a little forward in my chair.

'Why Louis the 16th of course! He and his family, a real plague, I'm telling you. They were a plague that needed to be stopped. And he, he was the worst, trust me. But luckily they did. They ended him.' he answered. It wasn't quite the answer I expected, though I couldn't say what I did expect.

'How did they end him?' I asked.

'Guillotine.' he said. I got silent. 'Did you have something to do with the plague? I saw the mask you were carrying when you came in. The same one as in the papers.' the man said rather happily.

'Yes, I used to be a plague doctor.' I said absently.

'Ha! Well, then you could have helped cure that plague of a family!' he burst out laughing. I hadn't heard anything of that French family before. I didn't know what to think of them, so I just laughed along. Hoping that he wouldn't notice it wasn't honest. I noticed Carlo did the same. 'You will find many people in Paris who hate Napoleon. Don't let them fool you.' the man said. He finished up his second glass of wine.

'They won't.' Carlo assured the man before I could start talking. We finished our glasses of wine in silence. We wished the man and lady a good night, walking towards the stairs. My legs were shaking underneath me as I went up, one stair at a time. When my head finally hit the pillow the pain left, allowing me to fall into a deep sleep.

CHAPTER 24

There was a bit of sunshine that got through the little window. The curtains hanging in front of it barely held back any light. Carlo was already up, sitting on the edge of his bed. He sat like a statue, staring at the window.

'Are you alright?' I asked him as I heard him grunt.

'Oh, hello. You're awake.' he said, still sounding a little sleepy. 'Yeah, I'm quite alright, just a little sore from the horse riding. It's going to be real fun once you try to get out of bed.' Carlo said. I hadn't gotten up yet, but I knew that he was right. I tried to get up as smoothly as possible. Wanting to show him it wouldn't bother me as much. It didn't go as expected. My muscles were so sore that I could barely straighten my back without making a sound. 'I told you.' Carlo said, laughing at me. My troubles seemed to make his less bad. 'You ready to continue riding?' he asked.

'Not one bit.' I grunted back. It took us so long to get ready. Our movements slow, in the hope that the pain would stay away. When we walked down the stairs we questioned if breakfast would still be an option. We sat down at the same table we had the night before. The table hadn't been set yet, but it didn't take long before the old lady came walking towards us with our food. Simple bread with cheese was presented to us, but we did not complain. We thanked the lady and began eating.

'We should leave some to take with us for lunch.' Carlo said.

'Yeah, alright.' I answered. Though we both thought it was a good idea, leaving any behind wasn't that much of a priority for us. We ate slice after slice until only a third of the bread was left. We packed the leftover bread and cheese together. We finished our glass of water and sat still for a moment. Neither of us wanted to get up. Both wanting this moment to last forever.

'I think we should get ready to leave.' I said after a while.

'Yes, we should.' Carlo answered. We both sat staring at one another. We sat for so long that the lady came back.

'Do you two want anything else?' She asked, hands hovering over our empty plates.

'No thank you, it was delicious. We should get going.' I said. I forced myself up from the chair. It took everything in me not to shout out when I did. I lowered my hand to Carlo and dragged him out of his chair. The lady found this very amusing.

Together we walked up the stairs. Even more slowly than we had the evening before. I felt the eyes of the lady burning on my back but didn't dare to turn around. So, slowly we got our stuff to leave. It took us what felt like hours to get all our stuff down. It really shouldn't have taken us so long, wasting most of our day.

When we were downstairs we thanked the lady once more for her kindness. The small man hadn't come out when we said our goodbyes.

When we set foot outside the inn the cold breeze hit us. The cold biting into our skin. We dragged our feet across the ground crossing the road to the field. The horses were still there despite the broken fence. They could have easily run away but didn't. Maybe they had been too tired to do so. I didn't blame them. We set out stuff against the fence and hopped over, which was more falling over the fence than anything else. We neared ourselves to the horses. They of course saw us and knew what was coming. So they did everything in their power to get away from us. We walked after them for a while. The horses were of course a lot faster than we could walk. After a while, it seemed like the fun had gone out of it for the horses, and they surrendered.

When we finally set off down the little trail in the forest half of the day had already slipped away.

We had been riding for quite some days now. This morning hitting the 12th. The mountains had definitely slowed us down. But now that the land was flat stretched out until the horizon once more, the days became easier. The horses were able to ride for more hours at a time. We began having fewer breaks and the breaks we did have became shorter. This all made the days go by a lot quicker. My legs still weren't all too happy with it. They had become a permanent sort of numb from all the riding. I spoke those concerns out to Carlo but it turned out he had the same problem.

We spent the evenings around a little fire that we would make. Heating up our bodies from the cold that tended to settle in at the end of the day. Stretching our legs on the grass. We would eat stale bread that we had gotten at a little village we had passed some days ago. We greatly missed the inn, as we had not stayed at another one after. It wasn't that we hadn't passed any possibilities. We agreed that it was better to save up the money that we had. Paris wasn't going to be cheap and we did really need a place to stay there. So with disappointment, we passed the inns, not looking back.

'How far are we from Paris?' Carlo asked. He sat on the grass, leaning against the saddle he had taken from the horse. He lay close to the fire for the warmth.

'A day or three. I think.' I answered. Staring at the flames in front of me.

'Okay.' Carlo grunted. 'I don't think my legs will work anymore once we're there. You might have to do the rest alone. I don't think I will ever take another step.' Carlo complained.

'Yes.' I simply said. I found that I wasn't truly listening to what Carlo was saying.

'What's the plan for when we get there anyways?' Carlo said as the shot up. This caught my attention.

'I thought you were the one making the plans?'

'Yeah, I am.' Carlo said proudly. 'I was just giving you a chance. I was thinking the first thing we do is sell these horses. Even if we don't stay for long, wanting to go back after this, these horses won't survive this travel once more. Plus, that will give us some much-needed money. That will secure us a room at an inn for at least three days. Even if it turns out Paris isn't the city we should be in, which I admit, I had almost forgotten. We need to rest for a bit.' Carlo said.

'I agree.' I muttered. I hoped Paris was the place we needed to be. I don't think I have much left in me to keep traveling from place to place, not knowing where I will end up.

'What are we looking for in Paris? We don't really have any clues telling us she's there, have we?' Carlo asked.

'No.' I answered softly. The reason we went to Paris was to go after Maximilien. Who is already dead? I wasn't sure what else there would be there that could help us any further. But I wasn't about to tell that to Carlo. Maybe I was letting Servius down. He would have known where to go, he would have told me what to do. But he didn't. 'I think we should talk to people, anyone. Try to figure out who Maximilien was.' I said, hoping that Carlo would accept it.

'That sounds about right. But even if we know who he was, what would that help?' Carlo asked. I looked at him. He was staring up. I followed his gaze and found myself looking at thousands of stars shining above me. I pondered over this question for a while.

'The bloody handkerchief!' I shouted out.

'I'm sorry?' Carlo said surprised. I picked up the suitcase that stood behind me. Kept at a good distance from the fire, as I did not want it to end up like the map had. I opened the suitcase. Rummaging inside, taking out the gourd that was hidden behind some spare clothing. I put the suitcase aside. Carlo stood up and made his way over to me. Settling down to the right of me, looking curiously at the object in my hands.

'What is it?' Carlo asked. I handed the gourd over to him. He turned it around in his hands. 'This isn't a handkerchief.' Carlo said carefully after some time. I took the gourd back from him, opening it up.

'The handkerchief is in the gourd.' I said, taking out the completely red handkerchief. I carefully handed it over to Carlo. He seemed a bit reluctant to take it.

'When you said "bloody handkerchief" I wasn't expecting an actual handkerchief drenched in blood.' Carlo said. His expression told me he wasn't all too fond of it. 'Do you think this is Servius's blood?' he asked.

'I don't know whose blood this is. That is what I would like to figure out. I think someone in Paris might know who it's from.' I said. I took the handkerchief back from Carlo, who gladly handed it over. I carefully placed it back inside the gourd.

'Sounds like a plan.' Carlo said.

We stopped our horses as something appeared on the horizon. There were two figures standing at a crossroad. At first, it seemed like they were going towards us, but they simply waited for us to get closer to them. I shared a concerned look with Carlo.

We had made many kilometers that day. The horses had strolled their way through the heat of the day. But because of their slow pace, breaks weren't needed as often. This had brought us a great deal closer to Paris. Closer to the answers I needed. But now there seemed to be an obstacle in front of us. Slowing down our pace.

It soon was presented to us that the two figures at the crossroad were soldiers. Covered in harnesses from top to bottom. Their weapons were bound to the saddle on which they sat. Ready for war. The horses underneath those saddles were enormous. We had to lift up our gaze to look the soldiers in the eyes.

'Well, hello you two.' one of them said once we had gotten close enough for them to start a conversation. 'What are you two up to?' he asked. We stopped the horses a good few meters away from them. The tone of his voice made it clear to be considered a threat. I didn't quite know how to respond. I wanted Carlo to answer, but the soldiers spoke in French. So it was my job to do the talking.

'We're making our way to Paris.' I replied. Hoping that leaving it as vague as possible will work in our favour. I was worried that this was it. That we had traveled all the way here, only to be stopped two days away from arriving at Paris.

'Are you assigned there?' the soldier asked.

'Assigned?' I said surprised, not sure what he was talking about. My horse started to get a little impatient, wanting to continue onward.

'Yes. Are you assigned to Paris? Or are you married?' the man said. His annoyance started to rise up.

'No sir, we're not married. What should we be assigned to?' I asked. Hoping that showing him respect would prevent him from becoming angry.

'The army of course! As citizens of France, you're assigned to the army! How could you possibly not know this!.' The shouted.

'Oh, but we're not from France sir. We are from Italy.' I told the man. I looked over at Carlo. He looked like he had seen a ghost. The shouting had really scared him.

'Are you now?' the soldier said. He made his horse take a few steps towards us.

'Yes, we can show you.' I said. I quickly opened the suitcase, taking out my papers. Maybe I hadn't been out in the world much, but Servius did well preparing me for it. I signed to Carlo to do the same. Both handed our papers to the soldier.

'Your friend here deaf?' the soldier spat at Carlo.

'He doesn't speak French.' I told the soldier. Carlo understood that we were talking about him. He forced a smile on his face and started nodding rather enthusiastically. The soldier examined our papers twice. Shifting his face between the papers and us. After a while, he handed them back. Seeming rather disappointed.

'Very well, you go ahead. You've wasted a lot of our time, come on, get out of here!' the soldier shouted. I quickly shoved the papers into my cloak. I set my horse to a quick canter and waved at Carlo to follow me. When we had made a good distance between us and the soldiers I turned around to see if they were looking at us. But when I turned around I found the horizon empty.

'I could follow that a little bit, but what was that about?' Carlo asked.

'They thought we were from France. Everyone in France is to be assigned to the army or something. Unless we were married.' I replied. My eyes still gazing at the horizon behind us, wondering where the soldiers had disappeared to.

'Kind of like the man at the inn told us.' Carlo said.

'Yes, indeed.' I said, turning my focus back to the road in front of us.

'Well, I'm glad that that is over. What is Napoleon doing that he needs so many soldiers? And desperately at that.' Carlo wondered out loud.

'Fighting a war. I mean, look at Rome. Rome was filled with French soldiers too. He is getting himself a bigger country.' I said. Carlo stayed silent. Now and then I shot a quick look behind us. Worried that the soldiers would reappear out of nothing.

The days after that were quite ordinary. Riding for a few hours, letting the horses rest, eat, and drink; then repeating the cycle. The riding had become increasingly dull once the mountains had passed. Just when we thought that we couldn't be any more bored, trouble started to arise.

'We are lost.' I said to Carlo. We were sort of lost. We had stopped following the drawn-out path a little while ago. Now we weren't so sure anymore of where we were. We had gone a little too much to the left. We marked a spot on the map, where we thought we were at the moment. We drew in a new route that we would take, hoping it would take us straight to Paris. There was a good chance that we could find Paris without the map. We just had to make some right turns, taking us back on the right road. But we didn't want to take the chance of getting even more lost. When we were sure that one way or another we would end up in Paris we continued our travels. Once we continued we didn't look at the map again.

We were about half a day away from reaching Paris. The pain in our legs had begun to settle down a bit. Not being as extreme as first, but it never truly faded away. When we thought we should have arrived we were met by an incredibly large building. It looked like a castle, without the towers reaching towards the sky. The building stood, surrounded by an enormous garden. The entire building, and everything surrounding it, seemed to be made out of gold. There were flags hanging with a logo on them that I knew all too well.

'Carlo.' I whispered. Carlo didn't notice and continued to stare at the large building. There were many soldiers standing all around the building. I drove my horse in between Carlo and the building. Grasping his attention. 'Carlo.' I whispered once more. Making sure the soldiers near the building wouldn't hear.

'Yes?' Carlo asked. He was whispering back to me, though he did not seem to understand why.

'Look at the flags.' I told him. Each flag was big in size. There was a golden eagle on each one of them. Surrounded by more golden details.

'Yeah. They're beautiful.' Carlo said. He was unsure of what I was getting at. I lowered my voice even more than I already had.

'Servius's ring has the same logo on it.' I told Carlo. He didn't seem all too shocked by this news.

'Are you sure?' He asked me. I nodded but didn't answer him any further. I quickened the pace of my horse. Getting us out of the soldiers's earshot as fast as possible. Once we were I slowed down my horse once more. Carlo did the same.

'Yes I'm sure, look.' I said, taking off my glove. I reached my hand towards Carlo. Carlo took my hand and examined the ring closely. 'Servius told me not to show it to anyone. That's why I hadn't shown you.' I said in an apologetic tone. The ring was big and held the exact same logo that was shown on the flags. Carlo's eyes widened.

'It is a good thing he told you not to show it to anyone. You better put your glove back on. Before anyone sees and asks you how you got that.' Carlo said. He pushed my hand back towards me and I put back on my glove.

'Maybe many people have a ring like this? To embrace the king.' I said.

'A ring that high of value? I don't think so.' Carlo answered. He nervously looked around him.

'We don't know how wealthy they are. Maybe most people can afford it.' I countered. After all neither of us had ever been in Paris. We didn't know how rich the people there were.

'Even if they have a good amount of money that ring is still expensive.' Carlo said. We rode further in silence. Pondering over the question.

* * *

We soon found ourselves at the edge of Paris. The streets were dirty, the smell stinging our noses and there were many people about who seemed to be sleeping outside. Their clothes were covered in dirt. They were slender, their ribs showing through their torn clothing. We rode through street after street that looked like this. I looked at Carlo. His face said enough. Not just everyone had such a ring.

CHAPTER 25

It wasn't just the outer layer of Paris that was filled with dirt. It was almost the entire city that looked like that. Most streets were filled with people wearing torn clothing, the grounds were covered in dirt. The smell throughout the city wasn't at all pleasant.

It all got a little better once we had gotten to the central part of the city. The houses there looked a lot better. Everyone was dressed in nice clean clothing and the bad smell of the streets around didn't reach there. The stables were placed in this inner circle. Something I hadn't expected. They weren't fully in the center of course, but it wasn't far from it.

There were three big stables connected to one another. There weren't any fields surrounding it, so the buildings were all it was. We got off our horses. Both stumbling once we hit the ground. The cramps that had slowly been decreasing came back all at once. Leaving me walking like an 80-year-old man. Carlo didn't seem to have the same problem. He wasn't walking as smoothly as he normally would, but it wasn't as bad for him. We led the horses to the most left of the three stables. We weren't sure if we were meant to go in there, but that was where most of the people were. No one knew us here. That much was clear. Each stable boy turned their head towards us when we approached. From what we could see most of the stables were empty. Occupied by a horse that wasn't there at the moment.

'Hi, we are looking to sell these horses.' I said. I waited for a moment. None of them seemed like they were going to answer me. 'The tack is included.' I added, hoping that that would get the attention of someone. It seemed to work. One of the stable boys came walking towards us.

'One moment. We will get the boss.' the boy said. He ran outside, towards one of the other two stables. Once he came back he was accompanied by a man walking with a cane. He slowly made his way towards us. I had already taken my belongings from the saddle. Carlo had done the same.

'Hello. We are looking to sell these horses. With their tack.' I said to the man. It was likely he knew what we were here for, but it seemed better to tell him again, just in case he didn't know. The man nodded.

He slowly made a little circle around the horses. Inspecting them with great care for detail.

'How much were you thinking to sell them for?' the man asked in a low voice. He spoke with a thick accent.

'What you find suiting for these two horses.' I replied. I knew this wasn't the smartest answer, but I wanted to be sure that we could sell the horses here. With my little knowledge of the currency here I didn't dare ask too much by accident. So I decided it was best to let him decide what we would get for them.

'5 francs.' he said in a disgusted tone.

'Well, for the horses, yes, but the tack is-,' I started, hoping that I could get the price a little higher.

'Well then how much were you thinking?' the man sneered at me. He clearly didn't find this very amusing.

'15 francs.' I said, knowing that this was rather much for the tack. The man laughed at me.

'10 is the highest I will go.' he said.

'Deal.' I said quickly, not testing my luck. I had gotten more than expected and that would be enough. The man grunted as he gave me the 20 francs. I nodded to Carlo to give the stable boy the horse. The moment the man handed me the money I wondered how much it really was. I should have asked the man at the inn how far one franc would get you. To have been better prepared for moments like these.

The stable clearly didn't like strangers. We quickly left the place, as the glances going our way weren't all too welcoming. We weren't too bothered by the fact that we left the stables quickly. We were both tired from our travels and wanted nothing more than to find a place to sleep.

After walking for a little while we found a street that was home to many inns. Each one competes with the others to get the most people. Colourful flags hang from the building. Blooming flowers outside. The doors were wide open, screaming "Come in!". Each inn we passed seemed to be fancier than the last.

Once we had walked through the entire street we decided to settle for the first one we walked past. Seeming to be the least fancy. Which hopefully meant that it would be cheap. At least cheap enough so that we could stay there.

Even though it was the least fancy of the street, didn't mean that it was looking as bad as the inn in Rome had. The door didn't creak when we opened it to enter. A warmer welcome we could not have hoped for. There were many people inside. All sitting around their own little round table. There were people playing music and everyone seemed to enjoy themselves. It wasn't necessarily a big inn, there were just many people inside. I began to doubt if they even had a room free. We walked up to the front desk. Carlo had taken over my suitcase so that I could easily get to my money.

'Afternoon.' said the man behind the desk. He was turned to watch the people playing music. The band consisted of a guitarist and a singer. I had heard better music, but it wasn't ugly. The man wasn't going to turn to look at us.

'Hello?' I asked. Raising my voice so that the man could hear it over the music. The man turned towards us. Seeming annoyed that we were taking his attention away from the music. He looked rather shocked when he saw us. He stumbled out of his stool, creating distance between us and him.

'What do you want?' he asked. There was a little bit of fear coming from his voice.

'We were wondering if you had a room left for us. For a few days if that is possible.' I answered. The man inspected us carefully. He was taking me in for quite a long time. Something I had gotten used to, but also forgotten during our time traveling.

'Why do you have that mask?' he spit out. I looked down at the mask in my hands. I had held it low in the hope that the man wouldn't have noticed. Perhaps if I had given it to Carlo the man wouldn't have.

'It is one of my personal belongings.' I said. The man laughed at this. The room around us had gotten silent. Everyone's eyes were pointed towards us. Nobody moved to make sure they were able to hear what we were going to say.

'Well, personal it is! I don't think anyone would want to share that with you!.' the man shouted. I was slowly losing my patience. I was used to people not liking me, but it was getting more and more annoying to deal with them.

'Is it, or is it not possible for us to get a room?' I asked, trying to keep my voice steady.

'Not with that mask no. You can go outside and throw it away, then come back. But not with it.' the man replied.

'Then we will leave.' I shot back. I turned around and signed to Carlo to follow me. Carlo gave me a glance that asked me what had happened. I shook my head to him to let him know I would tell him later.

'Do you enjoy it?' one man shouted from the back of the inn. I turned around, scanning the inn to see who had spoken.

'Enjoy what?' I asked, not able to find the man that had spoken. I wondered what the man had meant, but knew that I didn't really want to know.

'Making them sick! Killing people!' he spit out. The man stood up from where he had been sitting. The man was a little taller than me but didn't seem to have any muscles. He wore a nice suit. Making it clear to me that he wasn't used to hard work.

'You misunderstood. I am a plague doctor. From Venice. I work to make these people better. To cure the sickness they have. To heal them. Not to kill them.' I replied. The man looked around him, fear carved in his face, looking for backup.

'That is not what you've been doing! You have been walking amidst us people. The healthy ones. You have just been spreading the sickness so that you can kill more people!' the man shouted back at me. I wanted to shout too, but forced myself not to. Carlo shook my arm.

'Let's just get out of here, he is not worth it.' Carlo said. He started dragging me by the arm to the door of the inn. I should have walked out without saying anything else. But I simply couldn't. Servius wouldn't have accepted all that this man was saying about me. He would have stirred a little trouble. So I decided to stir some trouble. I grabbed Carlo's arm and pulled him back. I turned around to look at the man that had been yelling at me. I could see he had grown a little confident, thinking that I was leaving. I avoided Carlo's gaze as I knew he wouldn't be happy with what I was about to do.

'You might want to stay away from everyone for the next few days.' I started. Everyone in the inn held their breath. Surprised that I had spoken. I had much trouble hiding a grin. 'You are showing quite the number of symptoms of the plague. I would get some help if I were you.' I said. I nodded my head to him before leaving. We were not yet outside before I heard the chaos rise in the inn. It was clear that what I had said had scared the rest of the people inside. It became clear to me that the man whom I had been talking to was being driven outside. It was good to know that people were driven by fear. They had been one against me. Fear drove them to do it. But they all knew that I was a plague doctor. That meant to them that I was familiar with the plague. Something that is a greater fear to them than I could ever be.

'What did you say?' Carlo said, looking back at the inn. The man was being kicked out the door. Falling hard on the stones of the street.

'I just said that he was showing some symptoms of the plague.' I said. I couldn't help hiding my grin anymore. Carlo looked very pleased.

'Clever.' he said, holding in a laugh. We walked onwards, passing multiple inns. It was certain that we weren't welcome anymore in the inn that we had just left behind. That meant we had to find another place to stay. 'Did Servius teach you that?' Carlo asked.

'Yes, in a way. Servius used to make a little trouble now and then. Especially when someone treated him unfairly. I have taken over that trade from him.' I replied.

'I am sure he would be proud of you.' Carlo said. A simple sentence, though not one that I had expected. I imagined Servius standing next to us. He walked behind us. I turned around and saw him standing there. He nodded, accompanied by a smile on his face. Something that didn't happen often. Something destined for special occasions only. A warm rush of comfort filled my chest. Knowing that Servius was there. That he didn't think ill of me after all the mistakes that I had made.

'Shall we try this one?' Carlo asked. Dragging me back into reality.

'Sure.' I said. The inn was bigger than the one we had just left. Something that I didn't particularly like. There were two big doors that stood open, creating an entrance to what lay inside. The walls of the building were stone and the floor was covered by a carpet.

'Hello.' I said to the man who seemed like he could help us.

'What can I do for you two young gentlemen?' the man hadn't been much older than we were but acted like he had just passed the age of 70.

'We were wondering if you have a room left for two. For multiple days.' I said. The man inspected us. The other people inside hadn't bothered to stop what they were doing and look at us. We were completely invisible here. The man nodded, seeming eager to help us out. That look on his face didn't last long. The man saw the mask I was still holding and his gaze lingered. His eyes were filling themselves with fear.

'I would love to help, but I am afraid that were are fully booked.' the man said quickly. He hadn't looked anywhere to figure this out.

'Thank you.' I said and turned around. Carlo followed me outside. He had seen all that happened and knew that we weren't welcome here too.

'Maybe we should try a smaller inn. One that perhaps isn't all fancy.' Carlo said disappointedly.

'Agreed.' I replied. We walked down the road. Most of the inns on the road were bigger than the ones that we had just left and looked rather expensive. Giving a glance at the buildings made us believe that we would be sent out the moment we stepped foot in them. We dwelled off the road, trying to find a better inn elsewhere. After walking through a couple of streets we found a little inn. The door creaked as we opened it. The most welcoming sign that we could find. Maybe this was the place where we belonged.

CHAPTER 26

'Hello.' I said once more. It was getting late and we had entered many more inns looking for a place to stay. None of them wanted us there. During this day I had spoken more than I had in my entire life. I had never been this social. The man that sat in the big chair was reading a newspaper. He lowered the newspaper just enough so he could glance over it. He took a long time taking us in. We patiently waited for him to say something. His eyes met with the mask I was holding. The man quickly raised his newspaper once more and paid us no further attention.

'I was wondering if we could get a room here. For two people. For a night or three.' I said, hoping that the man would answer to this. The man didn't answer. He didn't even look up from his newspaper. We stood there for a moment unsure of what we had to do.

'Let's go. This won't work.' Carlo said after a little while. We left the inn, walking onto the nearly abandoned street outside. Carlo sighed and turned towards me. His eyes were filled with regret. The kind of regret you feel before you do something bad.

'I think you have to get rid of the mask.' Carlo said.

'What?' I asked in disbelief. He knew how much the mask meant to me. I had been carrying it for the entire journey. Now he simply wanted me to throw it away like it was a piece of trash.

'I know. But we don't really have any other choice, do we?' Carlo said carefully.

'Of course we have another choice! We will go into another inn to find a place to stay. And if they don't want us we will try another. One will want to take us.' I said. He couldn't expect me to throw the mask away. I wouldn't.

'No one will take us because of the mask.' Carlo said. He looked uncomfortably around him. I knew this was true.

'Maybe so, but I won't let go of it because of that.' I said. Carlo took me over to the side of the street. Getting out of sight of the three people that were occupying the street.

'Well, you have to. I know you don't want to let go of it. It's the last thing you have left of him. But it isn't him.' Carlo said carefully. He was talking so softly that even I had trouble hearing him.

'No, of course, it is not him. It is not the only thing I have left of him. He is still here, I have more than just the mask.' I replied. I knew I sounded upset.

'I understand. And I know that you do not simply want to throw it away. But you can't keep it. I'm sorry to tell you this, but the mask has been a burden. Even before this.' Carlo said. He held onto my right arm as if scared that I would run away.

'Servius has not been a burden!' I said rather loudly.

'No. Servius has not been a burden. He has been a great help. But the mask has been. As you said, the mask is not the only thing that you have left of him. He is still here. Leaving behind the mask won't change that. The part of Servius that was once in that mask will not be forgotten. You won't leave anything of Servius behind, he will always be with you. Letting go of that mask is the best thing you can do right now. The best thing we can do.' Carlo said. I weighed his words. I knew he was right. I needed to let go of the mask in order to continue. But saying it out loud wasn't so easy. Believing that nothing will go lost without the mask wasn't something I truly believed in yet. The object felt like a presence. Filling the void that Servius had once filled. Letting go of the mask may just make Servius a little smaller. Making him one step closer to being forgotten by me. The mask is a book in which all our memories lay. The Servius I knew had always been shown to be through the glasses of the mask.

I held up the mask. Looking at the broken glass. It had slowly gotten worse over time. Small pieces of glass falling out. It was now almost completely empty. Leaving nothing but a hole behind. It was broken. I was unable to ever use it again. The thought of using the mask again wasn't one I enjoyed. It was Servius I was holding onto, not Poveglia. During most of the journey getting here I had fantasised about going back to Poveglia. Homesick. To go back to the safe walls of the hospital. Where Servius would guide me through the days, telling me what was wrong and what was right. Listening to the stories of the patients. The routine of day-to-day life. Having a net that would catch me if I fell.

But now thinking about it the longing seemed lost. The desire to go back had faded. Only leaving the longing for clearance and acceptance. Something only Servius ever gave to me.

Carlo took his hand from my arm and put it on my shoulder.

'We don't know how long it will take us to find his wife. No matter how long it takes we will go through with it. But taking the mask along will only make it harder for us. It is time to let it go.' Carlo said. I knew Carlo was right. And for only a moment I accepted that this was my goodbye to the mask. I gave one last glance at the mask, before letting it fall out of my hands. I couldn't manage to set it down. Scared that the moment wouldn't last to the end of it. Scared that if I held on to it for just a moment longer I would never be able to let go. And so, the mask fell. It landed in a little puddle of what looked like water but didn't smell like it. It lay there on its side. The broken glass facing upwards.

CHAPTER 27

'Please, please don't leave me!' Fransisco pleaded. He sat on his knees in the dirt. 'Please don't go.' He cried out.

They were at the edge of the island. The waves were crashing into the side. There was heavy rain pouring down. Thunder rumbling in the near distance. The storm had been getting increasingly aggressive as the days passed by. The waves were getting greater. Some of them were high enough to get themselves on the island. The sky was filled with dark clouds. Even though it was in the middle of the day it was as dark as it is at midnight. Trees were swaying in the wind. Many branches had caved and were now lying in piles on the ground.

Fransisco forced his eyes open. He was completely drenched and his entire body was shivering. Despite the storm, Servius was determined to go to Venice.

'I have work to do.' Servius said sternly. He was disgusted by the boy on the ground. Crying because he didn't want to be left alone. Servius didn't look at the boy.

There was a little boat at the harbour that was moving rapidly over the waves. The man inside the boat clutched his hands to the sides, scared to fall into the water. Servius stood at the edge of the water. Fransisco looked hopefully through his tears. Hoping that Servius wouldn't go. That he would think better of it not to go out in the storm. Not to leave Fransisco behind.

Servius raised his foot. His eyes darted from place to place. Looking for the best way to enter the swaying boat. Fransisco got off his knees and ran towards the edge.

'Please don't do it! Please don't go! This isn't safe! Please just stay!' Fransisco cried out. He tugged at Servius's arm. Servius still didn't give the boy a glance. He reached forward with his foot and found the boat. As he did this he pushed Fransisco away. Fransisco lost his balance and fell down. Looking at Servius who had stepped into the boat. Servius seemed to have a lot less trouble with the swaying. His hands hidden in his cloak. Servius ordered the man to start rowing.

Fransisco sat there. In the mud in the pouring rain. Looking at the boat getting smaller. Tears were streaming down his face, though he couldn't tell how many.

'Please. I need you here.' He whispered.

CHAPTER 28

'Let's try another inn.' I said to Carlo. My voice cracked, but I didn't care. It felt like I had failed. I had let Servius go. Letting him fall onto the ground. Though the feeling of guilt crept up on me, there was also something that loosened. The mask had been a burden. A burden that weighed upon me more than I had thought.

When Carlo nodded I didn't think twice before walking away. I almost ran. I didn't want to be able to take back what I had done. I wanted to be able to let go. I wanted to believe that this wasn't an end. That things would go on, that nothing was lost. Carlo, who was surprised that I had run off so quickly put in a little sprint to get back to my side. We walked in silence for a while. Not knowing where to go, but not wanting to stay here.

The coolness of the evening began to set on us when Carlo had finally had enough of the silent walking.

'Okay, we have to find a place to sleep. I am tired and my legs are screaming.' Carlo said. I didn't answer him. I didn't even dare to look at him. Completely lost in my own thoughts. 'I think we will have the best chance at a small inn. One we haven't been to before.' Carlo added. Hoping that I would answer this time. Once it became clear to Carlo I would he began having a conversation with himself. 'We walked past one just now, didn't we? Yes, we did. I think we should try that one. Yes, I think we have a good shot there. But I need you to talk. Because, no matter how much I want to, I do not speak French.' Carlo said.

'Yes. Let's try that one.' I whispered. And so we turned around to find our way to the inn that we had just passed.

The inn that Carlo was talking about looked much like the one I had stayed at in Rome. The middle of the building was slightly caved in. Like a tree had fallen against it. Apart from the little board that hung above the door, the building was not screaming for attention. There wasn't even a proper door providing the entrance to the building. The so-called "door" was made of a few wooden planks that were put together. There wasn't a lock on it either. Surprisingly the door didn't creak as we opened it. There wasn't a bell that hung over the door either. Ringing to tell the person inside that someone had entered. Not that it mattered. There didn't seem to be anyone inside. Our footsteps echoed in the almost empty room.

There were a few paintings that hung on the wall and there were a few dead plants scattered around the room. There was a little round table in the corner of the room. On the table lay a book and pen to write with. There was a small chair standing next to the table that was missing some parts.

'Good evening gentlemen!' A loud singing voice came as a figure emerged from the stairs. 'Are you two looking for a room in one of the finest inns in Paris?' the man said beaming. He looked honestly proud of the building we were in. I wasn't sure how to reply to that, but luckily the man didn't let me reply. 'Because if you are, you are at the wrong inn! You will find those inns at the center, not here. But if you're looking for something cheap but comfortable, you're at the right address!' the man laughed. Normally the energy of the man would have leaked over to me, but now it didn't. Because the man was so happy I wondered if he would have cared about the mask. Guilt began to rise up as I answered the man.

'That is great. Exactly what we are looking for.' I said.

'Well isn't that amazing! What may I do for you?' the man said. The man was laughing at something funny that I didn't understand. I didn't laugh and Carlo only grinned stupidly, making the situation a little awkward. The man seemed less bothered by it than we had.

'We are looking for a room. A bed for each of us. We would like to stay for a few days, but we are not sure how many yet. But at least three.' I said. I put down my suitcase to free a hand, forgetting that the other was already empty.

'That is no problem! We have space for you here! You can share a room for two. It will be one franc per night. You can give me three now. You can stay longer after that, those costs will be paid once you leave. Doesn't that sound great!' the man said. All this time Carlo had been grinning. Perhaps it was meant to look kind and welcoming, but it looked rather creepy.

'That sounds good.' I said, feeling a little bad that I wasn't as excited as the man was. The man picked up the pen, hovering it over the book.

'What are your names?' the man asked.

'I am Fransisco, this here is Carlo.' I said. Carlo noticed that I was talking about him and started smiling even wider.

'Lovely.' the man said, writing something down in the book. When he was finished writing he bent down to look under the table.

Underneath the table stood multiple empty pots. It looked like they had been used before for plants that were now dead. The man searched around in the pots. When he reappeared from underneath the table he was holding a small key.

'So, you are from Italy?' the man asked as he handed over the key.

'Yes, we are. How did you know?' I said rather uncomfortably. I didn't know how safe it was to tell the man where we were from. He didn't seem to be all that dangerous, but I still wasn't fond of the idea of sharing any information about what we were up to.

'You here on a little honeymoon?' the man beamed. He didn't answer my question, but I was so surprised by this comment I completely forgot about it. I choked on my spit. I coughed twice before catching my breath. Carlo had no idea what was going on but seemed concerned.

'Oh no. We are just friends.' I said.

'Oh don't worry about it. I know that many other people wouldn't be okay with it. But it doesn't matter to me!' the man said, smiling ever wider than Carlo had.

'We are really not-,' I started but the man cut me off.

'You look like a good happy couple.' the man said. I didn't know what about the sighting of us told him that, but it was something I couldn't see. He smiled at Carlo, and Carlo smiled back. Something he shouldn't have done, as it seemed the man saw that as a conformation. 'Your room is upstairs. Have fun!' the man said, raising his hand to point to the stairs. I didn't say anything as I picked up my suitcase and walked up the stairs completely astonished. Carlo followed me.

'Are you okay?' Carlo asked as we were walking through the hallway upstairs.

'Yes.' I said as I examined the key. There was a little number one pressed into the key. There were only four rooms in the building so it wasn't too difficult to figure out which one was room number one.

'What was it about?' Carlo asked further. Seeming very interested in what had been said.

'Oh, nothing. He just thought that we were on a honeymoon.' I reluctantly replied. The moment the words had left my mouth Carlo burst out in laughter. His laughter bounced through the entire hallway. I nervously looked around to see if the man was near. Carlo was laughing so loudly that it didn't really matter where the man had been. 'It is not that funny.' I said in an attempt to get him to stop laughing. This only seemed to make it more funnier for Carlo, who was now lying on the floor from laughing. I quickly opened the door to our room and stepped in. I turned around to close the door in Carlo's face but he was too quick and stopped me.

'No, perhaps not. But your reaction was.' Carlo said in between chuckles. 'And besides I have a way better taste than what you are.' he said. Which was so funny to him that it started another burst of laughter.

'Well thank you.' I said as I set down my suitcase. The room only had one bed in it, but I didn't want to go back down to ask for a different room. I lay down on the bed. Carlo, completely taken over by laughing didn't make it to the bed. He was back on the floor. I couldn't help but start laughing myself as I lay there, listening to Carlo. So together we laughed for what seemed like hours. I wondered what the man would be thinking of us. Whatever he thought was happening probably didn't even remotely look like the sad situation that was unfolding in the room. After a while, I had gotten too tired to continue laughing. Listening to Carlo's chuckling that slowly died away in the background.

CHAPTER 29

I awoke much later. The light from the sun outside shone through the small window. The noise from all the people outside told me that it was much later than morning. Carlo had made it off the floor and was still sleeping beside me. The noise outside made me curious, but I didn't want to wake Carlo up. I took the bottle with ash out of my cloak and put it down on the little nightstand. It would be safer to keep it here. I threw my cloak on the ground, tired of having to carry the weight of it on my shoulders.

I sat on the edge of the bed. Looking at the bottle. The ash seemed to be stuck together, forming one big rock. Servius had become so little. A man that once could never be put down now could be blown away with the slightest breeze. I sat there for a while, but Carlo did not wake up.

I took a small piece of paper and wrote "I am out, will be back soon." and left it on his nightstand.

I quietly made my way outside. The air was rather chilly. Hiding the fact that the winter had passed and the summer was coming. It had been much colder in France than it had been in Italy. Something that I found quite pleasant. The sun hid away behind a cloud now and then. Most of the people around me were hiding in thick jackets. I walked through the streets, following the outer ring for a while before heading to the center. Even though many people lived in the city of Paris, there were many trees and plants. It made the city a lot more pleasant. It didn't make the city less human-like, as every plant had been placed strategically. Standing in a pattern, not one bit overgrown.

When I got to the center of the city there were loads of people shouting and running about. There were people walking towards me from all sides. Soon I found myself in the middle of a group of people. All chanting the same words. There were too many people around me. Too many people that I didn't know. Shuffling against me, dragging me with them. I didn't know where they were taking me. Where they were going. I looked around me, hoping to see Carlo, but of course he wasn't there. I kept turning around, finding my balance so to keep me from getting under everyone's feet.

When there was a tiny gap in the stream of people I saw him

standing there, at the end of the street. The figure in the black cloak. Holding a dirty broken plague mask in his hands. He wasn't happy with it. I had made a mistake. He believed that I would take care of him, but I didn't. Servius. I had to get to him, I had to make right what I did wrong. I had made a mistake. I had done something I never wanted to, but had to. Because of someone else. I lost my true self because I acted not for me, but for someone else. Servius had warned me about it.

But I knew it wasn't him standing there. Not truly him. I had burned his body. The ash was in the little bottle that stood on the nightstand in the room at the inn. That was where Servius was. Not here in the crowd. I understood that but didn't quite believe it. Panic started to rise in me. Scared to lose myself like I had in Rome. I had to get out of here before I was somewhere else. Before I would be back on Poveglia. The island that had once seemed like home now looked so dreadful.

I shoved people to the side, making my way to where I had come from. I didn't look at the ones I shoved, nor did I apologize to them. All I wanted was to get out of the crowd. To get somewhere quiet. Somewhere I could breathe.

When I had managed to squirm my way to the street I had come from I turned around one last time. Servius was gone, but I knew that wasn't for forever. Servius was here. There was a piece of him here, a piece that I needed to find. I almost started running back towards the inn, but stopped myself. Running wouldn't do the situation any good. I forced myself to walk back.

The inn was just as broken as it had been when we saw it first the day before. It was easy to find between the nice houses that occupied the rest of the street. When I entered the same man as the night before sat at the table. He held a glass of wine in his hand examining me as I entered. Like he had already forgotten who I was.

'Good afternoon.' I managed to get out.

'Good afternoon indeed! Had a fun night?' the man asked. Sounding just as cheerful as he had last night. I knew what he was getting at. I wanted to tell him once more that we weren't a couple, but knew he wouldn't believe it.

'Yes, a good night's sleep. He is still asleep now. I think I better go wake him up before the day is gone.' I said as I began running up the stairs. The man said something to me but I didn't hear it. I tried to open the door but my hands moved too quickly. I struggled a while before the door was opened by Carlo.

'Everything alright? Last time I checked it wasn't that difficult to open a door.' Carlo said. He looked as if I had just woken him up. However, when I looked behind him I saw that the piece of paper I had laid out for him had been moved.

'Yes, we have to go.' I said to Carlo. Forcing myself through the doorway.

'Like, get out of this place, or go outside?' Carlo asked confused.

'Go outside.' I said. I took my cloak and started to put it on swiftly. I took the bottle of ash and put it in my pocket.

'Are you going to tell me why we are in a hurry?' Carlo asked, jumping around as he tried to get on his shoes. I waited impatiently in the doorway.

'I saw Servius.' I said. Carlo stopped jumping around. Still holding one foot up in the air.

'You saw Servius?' he asked like I was going crazy. I knew that he thought I meant it. That I believed that I had seen the living Servius.

'No, not the living Servius. I know he wasn't really there. But I saw him like I had in the art gallery in Rome. I want to go back and see if there is a part of him there. Maybe we can figure out who his wife is. Last time I found you, which helped me further. It may be the same now.' I said. Carlo put down his foot and looked at me. He put on his jacket, though moved a lot less quickly.

'Why didn't you figure it out while you were there?' Carlo asked.

'Well, you know what happened in Rome. And besides, there are way too many people outside.' I replied. Carlo nodded at me and followed me out the door. The man in the chair waved at us as we passed him. I didn't, but Carlo waved back. I led Carlo to the place where I had seen Servius.

We had gotten closer to the center of Paris when the chanting began to get louder. The streets were slowly becoming busier. There were people holding pieces of paper with words on them up to the sky. There were tables and desks stacked together, on which people stood, speaking to the crowd beneath them. Their voices carried over the shouting. There were soldiers standing on multiple spots in the streets. Soldiers that I hadn't seen before. Trying to keep what was happening in front of them under control. We stayed at a good distance from the protest for a bit.

'I don't think it is a good idea to be here.' Carlo said nervously.

'I know it isn't the best idea, but we have to figure out more.' I said, having to raise my voice so that Carlo could hear.

'How are we going to do that?' Carlo asked. I looked at one of the men standing on the pile of tables. I started making my way through the wall of people. Forcing myself closer to him. "Napoleon is weak! He should keep fighting, not give up! We will win!." the man was shouting. The people around him were howling, praising his words. The man on the tables took it in with pride before shouting the same words once more.

'I have a plan.' I said to Carlo, though I was sure he couldn't hear me. I took him by the arm and dragged him with me the last few meters. Making sure I wouldn't lose him. We finally made it through all the people, being less than a meter away from the man on the table. I wasn't sure how I would get out of this, but that was a problem for later.

'What do you know about Maximilien?' I shouted to the man. Carlo tugged at my arm, worried by what I had just done. The man up on the table hadn't heard me, but the woman beside me did.

'Maximilien?' the woman spit out. She seemed to want to answer but didn't want to miss what was going on in front of her at the same time. 'He was a political man or something. Something with the French Revolution. He made people who were against it meet the guillotine I believe. He has caused many deaths.' she shouted. She didn't wait for my thank you as she began howling at the man on the table. I dragged Carlo to the side.

'Okay, hear me out. We will go back into that crowd. We will go somewhere where there are fewer people, but still one of those leaders. We will ask them what they think of Maximilien and if his actions weren't better.' I shouted at Carlo. He didn't seem too convinced but nodded nonetheless.

'I see a lot of ways that this could go wrong.' Carlo said as I wanted to walk away.

'We don't really have another plan now, do we?' I said

'Yeah well, I do think that we could figure something out that won't possibly lead to our deaths.' Carlo said, looking at the mass of people around us that was still growing.

'I think we will be fine. It is a big group, but a large city. If there arise any dangers I am sure we will find a way to escape.' I said to Carlo.

'Okay. Say the plan goes right and we don't get killed. What will we do with that information?' Carlo asked. He really didn't like the idea.

'We will know who Maximilian truly is. We will know if people liked him or not. Maybe we can figure out where he is from.' I replied.

'I can tell you that.' Carlo said. My eyes got wide.

'Really?' I gasped.

'Yes, I told you before. He is dead.' Carlo said.

'Oh.' I answered, not quite happy with the answer that he had given me.

'But maybe he has children?' Carlo added.

'Great.' I shouted. I didn't give him time to say anything else. I didn't want to hear how that would be a very small chance. And that if he had it wouldn't mean that they were alive and well, still living in Paris. 'So we will figure out who they are and where they live. We will go back to the room, take the gourd and go to them. They will have to know more about it.' I said cheerfully.

'Will they know more about it?' Carlo doubted.

'I don't know. But it is the best we can do for now.' I said. Carlo didn't look assured by this. I wasn't too assured by it either, but it was the only plan we had. 'You have made the last plan, let me take it from here.' I said confidently.

'Okay. We will follow your plan. But if it takes us to danger I will take over. And we will never follow your plan ever again. Okay?' Carlo said.

'Okay.' I replied. We made our way back into the dense crowd. My eyes were ringing from all the shouting, that came from everywhere around me. We left the center, as there was no way to find a smaller group there. There were loads of smaller groups just out of the center. Though there were many smaller groups, many of them consisted of big muscled men. I didn't doubt the plan as much as Carlo, but I still wanted to prevent a fight.

After walking through the streets for a while we found a suitable small group. They were dressed in nice clothing and didn't seem like they were looking for a fight. They were shouting like the rest of the people but in a much more mannered way. There was a possibility that they didn't want to talk to us, but it was worth a shot. I signed at Carlo to follow me.

'Hello.' I started but didn't wait for the man to answer. 'What do you think of Maximilien?' I asked. I wasn't looking for any small talk and they didn't seem to be either.

'Maximilien?' one of the men asked. A question I hadn't thought of.

'Maximilien Robespierre.' I replied. Hoping that they knew who I was talking about.

'That man was a killer. Yes, he was for the revolution, but killing isn't the way to win.' another man said.

'Did he kill that many people?' I asked. I was certain that there was a connection between him and Servius. Something I just didn't know yet. But that he was a killer explained the bloody handkerchief.

'If someone was against the revolution, or if he thought they were against it, he threw them in the guillotine. A madman if you ask me. I am glad they executed him.' the man said.

'They should have executed the entire family.' another man added. The man who had spoken before looked at him with a questionable gaze. 'What? If one in the family is bad it almost certainly means the entire family is crazy. They are a danger to us!' the man said to defend himself.

'There are family members left?' I asked. Hoping not to seem too eager.

'Yes, his daughters. Charlotte and Henriette, I believe are their names. They live in Paris, easy to track down. Most people choose to ignore them. They believed that Maximilian was the only rotten apple in that family.' the man said. This was exactly what we needed. Those were the people who would give us answers.

'Do you happen to know where they live?' I asked.

CHAPTER 30

We made our way back to the room. Most of the streets were now filled with people. We took a little longer getting back to the inn, having to make our way through them. Even in front of the inn stood a group of people. However, that was not the reason why they were there. When we walked in the man was still sitting in the same spot as he had before. His nose now behind a newspaper. The glass of wine was now empty and stood on the floor.

'Was it fun out there? I hear a lot of shouting. Another protest I assume. Happens a lot these days.' the man said cheerfully. He lowered his newspaper to get a good look at us.

'Yes, it was great fun. We are just taking a quick break before going out again.' I answered while making my way to the stairs.

'Alright! Be careful with the protests. It can become quite dangerous.' the man said. Bringing his attention back to the newspaper in his hands.

'We sure will.' I replied. Carlo didn't ask me to translate the conversation, but I did it anyway.

'Why do you think these protests happen often?' Carlo asked. I searched my pockets for the key.

'I don't know.' I answered. I found the key and quickly opened the door. 'We know it had something to do with Napoleon. Maybe the man downstairs knows what is going on. We could ask him.' I said.

'Yes.' Carlo answered. I took my suitcase from the floor and placed it on the bed. I opened it and took out the wooden gourd. The handkerchief was still safe inside it. I closed the gourd and put it in my cloak. The gourd itself wasn't that big, but the weight pulled down my cloak. I didn't want to have to carry it in my hands, so this was the best I could do. Carlo waited until I was ready. We left the room once more together. We locked the door and went downstairs where the man still hadn't moved.

'Do you happen to know why there are so many protests?' I asked the man. He dropped his paper and smiled widely. Happy to have someone to talk to.

'Yes. There is talk of Napoleon losing his position as ruler. He has lost a battle and now he has to leave the throne.' the man said.

'Thank you.' I replied. The man nodded. He gloomily picked up his newspaper as we left the inn. I translated what had been said to Carlo.

'Well, that does explain the protests.' Carlo said.

'Yes, it does.' I answered. Looking around at everyone on the street.

'I don't think that had anything to do with Servius.' Carlo pondered.

'No, I don't think so either.' I replied.

The house that stood on the address that we had gotten was rather small compared to the houses surrounding it. There was a little alleyway placed to the left of the house. when we looked at it we were surprised to see it didn't lead anywhere. The house was in good condition. All windows were blocked by curtains, making us unable to see inside. The door to the house was painted bright red, which made it stand out against the dull grey colour of the bricks.

'This is it?' Carlo asked.

'Yeah.' I said. I knew why he was doubtful of the fact. I had expected it to be bigger. Maybe putting people in the guillotine didn't pay so well after all. I walked through the front yard, which was no bigger than two meters, to get to the door.

'Hang on!' Carlo shouted. 'What are we going to say? What if they don't want us here? We are strangers you know. We can't force them to talk to us.' Carlo said.

'Well, there is only one way to find out, isn't there? I will knock and we will just wait. See if anybody is home. Then if they do open the door we will ask them if they are the daughter of Maximilien. And if they say yes we will ask them a few more questions. If they are reluctant we will show them the gourd. Maybe that will convince them.' I told Carlo. I hoped I sounded confident, as that was something I was quite lacking at the moment. Carlo stood close by me as I knocked on the door. I had knocked softer than expected so I knocked once more a little harder. There weren't any sounds coming from inside. I took a step back and waited for a moment.

'I don't think anyone is here.' Carlo said.

'Let's try once more.' I replied. I took a step closer to the door and knocked once more; even harder this time. There was a soft shuffling noise coming from inside the house. I had barely taken a step back when the door opened just a little.

'What do you want?' And an elderly woman spit out.

'Hello. We were wondering if you were the daughter of Maximilien

Robespierre.' I asked. Though I didn't know how long ago it was that Maximilien had died, she seemed to be a little old to be his daughter.

'No, I am not. But those two do live here, yes. If you came here to threaten them you have wasted your time. You are not the first one and I won't have it again!' the woman said sternly.

'We are not here to threaten them. We hoped we could ask them a few questions about Maximilien. About his artistic days.' I said, not sure if I should bring up the gourd immediately.

'Funny way to talk about his beheadings. If you think that we approve of what he did you are wrong. Now get lost!' the woman shouted as she started closing the door.

'Wait!' I shouted back. I hadn't expected it to work but the woman reopened the door a little.

'What?' she asked. I couldn't tell if she was pleased by us not giving up so quickly or not. I took the wooden gourd out of my pocket and showed it to her.

'Maximilien made this. Do you happen to know anything about it?' I asked her. The woman inspected the gourd for a little. Something in her face changed.

'Go somewhere else with your jokes.' she said, slamming the door in our face. Carlo and I stared at each other for a little while.

'So much for answering our questions.' Carlo said while looking at the gourd. He turned around and walked away from the house. He had already crossed the street before I had turned around. I ran after him.

'Okay. I admit, this didn't go as planned. But there is still hope.' I said as I tried to keep up with Carlo. He was walking over to one of the benches further down the street. The house was located near a little park area, where Carlo and I sat down. I still held the gourd in my hands and inspected it once more. There wasn't anything new to it that I hadn't seen before.

'Hello?' A soft voice spoke. When I looked up there was a young woman standing in front of us. She was wearing a floral dress. Her eyes were green and she had dark brown hair. Carlo hadn't noticed her coming either. 'I overheard your conversation at the door.' she said, as neither of us replied to her greeting.

'Hello.' I said. I saw that Carlo wanted to answer, but didn't know what to say.

'I am Henriette, the daughter of Maximilien.' she said. I shot up and looked at her hopefully.

'You are?' I asked. A rather stupid question.

'Yes. I am sorry about my aunt. She isn't very fond of people. I don't blame her. We have gotten a lot of people at our door. Threatening us. But anyway, that is not important. You wanted to ask me some questions about my father?' she said. She was looking rather uncomfortably around her. Not completely trusting us.

'Yes. This gourd.' I said, holding up the gourd to her. She took it in her hands. She turned it around and read the text on the bottom. 'Your father made this. Do you happen to know why and do you know whose blood is on the handkerchief?' I asked. She looked up at me, her eyes wide open.

'Blood?' she asked nervously.

'Yes. There is a handkerchief inside that is soaked in blood, look.' I said as I took back the gourd. Turning the gourd around, revealing the bloody handkerchief hidden inside. She took back the gourd, but not the handkerchief.

'Well, it says here that it is the blood of King Louis XVI.' she said, pointing to the backside of the gourd. I positioned myself next to her. There, at the bottom of the gourd was a slight cut in the wood. I hadn't been able to read it myself. Thinking nothing important was written there. But now that Henriette had pointed out there was something written there, I saw it too.

'But that is very unlikely isn't it?' I gasped.

'Yes. But that is what it says. I knew my father was working on this. The gourd. But I never asked him why he was making it. But I know that he was there when the king got beheaded. So it is possible.' she said. I looked at Carlo. I knew that he didn't understand what was being said, but the surprise that it had given me couldn't be missed.

'Do you know why he sent it away afterward?' I asked.

'I saw him give it to someone. Said it was meant to go to Venice or something. I don't know who he would give the blood of the kind to. Seems like a weird present.' she replied. She handed the gourd back over to me.

'Did he tell you the name of the person to whom he was sending it?' I asked.

'He didn't exactly tell me. I rather overheard it. The person whom he gave it to had the task of bringing it to Venice. He seemed to know where to go.' she said. It was meant for Servius. There was no other explanation as to why he had it.

'Thank you.' I said. Even though we didn't have the answers to everything, she had helped us a great deal. I still didn't know who Servius's wife was.

'He did say something about someone in Paris. She also knew where the gourd had to go to. They said something about needing to punish her.' she whispered. She looked as if she felt bad for not having more information that we needed. But what she had given us was more than we had before.

'What was her name?' I asked.

'Rosalie. I believe she used to work for the king. She fled off to a cemetery when he was killed. Cemetery Madeleine, I believe. She works there now.' She answered.

'Thank you!' I beamed with excitement. I was ready to turn around and translate for Carlo when she spoke once more.

'You know. There has been some talk about the beheading. Some say that it wasn't the king inside the guillotine. But someone else. I wasn't at the beheading myself. My father didn't want me to. So I didn't see it for myself. If it wasn't the king, I don't know who else it could have been.' She said.

'Did the name Servius ever come up?' I asked. It was worth a shot. Carlo had heard the name and listened eagerly. Henriette thought for a moment.

'He did sign some letters to someone named Servius. From Italy as well I think. Never asked him about it.' she said. So Maximilien was the person sending letters to Servius. 'But I must be going now. Before my aunt notices I have been talking to you.' she said with a smile. She nodded us goodbye before she ran off.

'Are you going to translate that for me?' Carlo asked desperately. I had been staring at the gourd, lost in thoughts, and had totally forgotten about him.

'Yes, of course. Maximilien was the person, or one of the people, who wrote to Servius. He helped execute the king, Louis the 16th, whose blood was in the handkerchief. There were some rumours about it not being the king who was beheaded. But if it wasn't the king she didn't know who else it could be. There was a person who knew about the gourd. Her name is Rosalie. She used to work for the king but now works at cemetery Madeleine. We have to get there. There is a good chance she will know more about Servius.' I translated.

'Sounds like a plan.' Carlo said. I stood, ready to start walking, but

Carlo didn't follow me.

'Are you coming?' I asked.

'Are you sure about this?' Carlo replied.

'About what? I know that she wasn't that old when the beheadings took place, but I think she still told us the truth. There is no reason for us not to believe her.' I answered. I was taken aback that Carlo was questioning what had been told to us.

'I am not talking about Henriette. I don't have any doubts about her. I am talking about Servius. When we go there. If Rosalie will be able to help us further. You will get to know things about Servius you hadn't before. Things that may be bad. Do you truly want to know who he was?' Carlo said.

'What? Are you going to tell me now you knew who he was all along?' I asked. Carlo laughed at this.

'No. I don't know who he was. But everything that has become clear has, how weird it may seem, led to the king of France. What if he is the son of the king? What if he had been working for the king? I am just asking if you have thought about getting to know all of Servius.' Carlo said. His voice sounded sincere. I had never thought about not wanting to know who Servius was. Besides it was more than just getting to know who he was. I had a task at hand.

'Why would it matter? Even if he was the son of the king it wouldn't matter. Servius is Servius to me. That will always stay that way. That won't change because of who he was before he became a doctor. Before I met him. Besides, I highly doubt him being royal blood. Those people are ignorant, nothing like Servius.' I replied. Carlo raised his shoulder.

'If you want to, that's good. I just wanted to make sure that you knew what may lay ahead. I know you care about Servius. I wouldn't want you to lose that.' Carlo said.

'Why would I see him any differently?' I asked Carlo. He knew less about Servius than I did. He didn't have a full picture, a complete person in front of him.

'Because you do not always have control over that. I didn't mean it in a bad way. There is nothing you can do about it, but to prevent.' Carlo said. He waited a moment for me to say something. I didn't know what to say, so I stayed silent. 'Now let's find a way to the cemetery. Madeleine was it?' Carlo said.

'Yes.' I said. I turned around to walk away but Carlo stopped me.

'Maybe we should go back to the inn and ask the man where it is rather than to search the entire city. My legs are still a bit sore. I don't think they would survive that.' Carlo said.

'Sound like a plan.' I replied as I followed him onto the road back to the inn.

CHAPTER 31

'Cemetery Madeleine?' the man asked. 'I know where that is.' he said, though he didn't sound all that confident. He bowed over the table. Searching through a pile that contained every single object that you could think of, until he found a map of Paris. He spread it out on the table. 'This is where we are now.' the man muttered. He pointed at a spot on the west of the map. 'And this is where the cemetery is.' he beamed. Pointing to the north, just a little higher than the center.

'Thank you.' I said as I had already turned around to walk out of the door. Carlo followed me. 'Let's get there fast.' I said. I didn't look at Carlo as I spoke, but knew he was following closely. He had been following me from the start of the journey. There wasn't a thing that made me believe he wasn't now. The center of Paris was still filled with a large amount of people. The protests were still going on. We chose to walk a little around the center, to avoid the worst of it. It took us a while, with getting lost a few times. During the time we had been walking through the streets, it had started to rain. It was pouring down as we turned the corner to the last street. I couldn't help but think of the plague mask. That was lying somewhere in the pouring rain. It wouldn't be able to handle the rain. It would be destroyed if it had not been yet. It hurt me to think of it. If I would have taken it with me, taken care of it, it would still be fine. But sometimes we can't take care of something we care about so much. I had to let go of the mask. I physically did, but mentally not.

'Is it here?' Carlo asked as we walked down the street.

'I think so.' I said. My pace had slowed down the past two streets. I had become unsure of what I was about to do. Unsure about the actions I would take, with the consequences that would follow. I had replayed Carlo's words over and over in my head. Maybe I didn't really want to know who Servius was. I tried to deny it, but I knew too that I would see Servius differently after this.

The bottle in my cloak hit the side of my stomach. I had made a promise. I would bring his ashes and ring to his wife. Something that couldn't be done without figuring out who Servius really is. So I had to come to terms with the fact that I would see Servius differently. Servius had known that this was going to happen. Which hadn't stopped him from sending me towards it. This was something I could not avoid.

CHAPTER 32

Servius stood near the edge of the water. A black silhouette against the setting sun. His cloak calmly waving in the wind. Which was the only movement he made.

Fransisco stood a good bit behind Servius. Trying to hide in the shadows of the tree. He looked at Servius. There was an odd sense of fury flowing through him. He couldn't believe Servius would make him do that. Fransisco pushed away the stiffness of his anger and moved towards Servius. The leaves under his feet crumbled as he made his way over. Servius had of course heard him coming but didn't turn around to greet him.

Fransisco thought about pushing him into the water but thought better of it not to. He stood beside Servius at the edge, looking at the setting sun rather than at Servius. The wind seemed stronger at the edge and a chill crept over his spine. It had been a dreary day, of which most he had spent inside. He tightened his cloak around himself. They stood there for a moment. Neither one of them said anything. Fransisco knew he was the one who ought to speak first but wasn't sure where to start.

'I didn't want to do it.' he said after a while. The words were barely audible over the crying wind and crashing waves. Fransisco hoped Servius hadn't heard. Because at once the words had sounded rather stupid to him. Servius didn't look at him as he answered.

'What exactly?'

'Burning my dad.' Fransisco said. 'I didn't want to do it. But you made me.' At this, Servius shifted his gaze at him. Like he was surprised that Fransisco would say that.

'I don't believe I made you do it.' he said. Fransisco took a deep breath. Trying to settle the anger he felt.

'You ordered me to start the fire. You made me do it.' Servius nodded.

'I did order you to start the fire yes. But it's hardly my fault that that is what you did.' I looked at him. He sensed my confusion and continued on. 'I didn't take your hand and forced you. I told you what to do and you chose to follow my command.'

'What else was I supposed to do?'

'To not.'

'So I should have ignored your orders?' I said, no longer hiding my anger.

'Yes. If you believed that it wasn't your job to start that fire, if you really

didn't want to do it, then why did you?'

'Because you told me to.' I answered. Sounding a lot more certain of this than I felt. Servius shook his head.

'While I greatly appreciate you trying to keep up my appearance, of having to do what I say,' he started 'I do believe that you have your own brain. You stand alongside me Fransisco, not underneath me. I assumed you knew.' Fransisco got silent.

'We are equal?'

'You sound surprised.' Fransisco looked at Servius, who seemed too busy with the sunset to look back at him. Fransisco never viewed himself as equal to Servius, nor did he think Servius did. 'What was the real reason you didn't want to do it? Why are you really mad at me?' Fransisco wanted to protest that he wasn't angry at Servius but stopped himself. He was, and if Servius wanted him to speak his mind he would. Besides, Servius wasn't stupid and had noticed from that day that Fransisco had been mad at him.

'You made me a monster.'

'Excuse me?' Servius said questioning.

'You made me burn him, you made me a monster.' Servius turned himself towards Fransisco.

'Why does that make you a monster?'

'He is gone because of me. I made him into nothingness.'

'I do believe that he was gone before you burned him. Burning bodies doesn't make you a monster.'

'But you're getting rid of them' Fransisco said before Servius could continue. Servius thought about this.

'I don't believe you're really getting rid of them, are you? If you wanted to get rid of them you would just dump their body in the sea and call it a day. I see burning as a proper goodbye. You take away the tomb of the soul. Taking away all doubt that the soul is free. So the soul doesn't question whether it is free to roam or perhaps the body isn't quite dead yet and it should stay. You're giving peace to the dead.'

'I don't think that's how other people see it.' Fransisco said. Servius laughed at this.

'Of course not. All other people see are monsters who burn people.' Fransisco looked at Servius. As to say "See, so we are monsters!" Servius did not meet Fransisco's eye as he continued. 'But they don't know the full story. They're too blinded by grief or fear to truly see what is going on. We shouldn't be filled with grief, and certainly not with fear. If you are, then I'm afraid you're a monster in many more ways than one.'

CHAPTER 33

The cemetery wasn't that big. There stood a little church. Next to the church were two lines along which lay graves. The graves were decorated with what seemed like little roofs. Each grave being protected from the rain. I walked through the big gate that led to the church. It made me a little uneasy that such a little church was protected by such a large fence.

There were flowers planted along the main path of the cemetery. Making the gloomy place shimmer with a little bit of hope. We never planted flowers near the graves on Poveglia. Though other plants liked to take their roots near them. It seemed nice. Planting flowers in a place so dark. Maybe I would go back to Poveglia. To plant a flower there. I knew I probably wouldn't, but it was a nice thought to have. I reached for a flower, holding it in between two fingers for a little while. Admiring its beauty. My hands were shaking a bit from the cold. I had been drenched entirely by the rain.

'Fransisco.' Carlo said softly, pointing to a grave. It was the grave of King Louis the 16th. Next to the king lay two other people that I didn't know of. Neither did Carlo. The rain had become too heavy to clearly read the letters on the stones.

'Let's go inside. I said. Carlo agreed and together we entered the little church. The rain stopped hitting our faces, the moment we reached the front door. The entry to the church was a rather small door. Carlo stopped me before I could open it.

'Do you want me to wait outside for you?' he asked.

'No. You've come all this way with me. And besides, there is a good chance that we won't figure out who he is yet. So there is no need for you to get all... whatever you are. You wouldn't even understand the conversation.' I said smiling and entered the little church. Inside, the church was almost completely empty. There were a few candles and pews, but nothing more than that. There weren't any statues or paintings. The only decoration there was were the patterns on the walls.

There were three women standing together in a circle. They all looked around as we entered the church. Each one of them wore a black cloak. Not like the one that I was wearing. One that had a religious purpose.

'Hello.' I whispered, not sure if I was allowed to talk or not. I made my way to them as quietly as possible. Leaving a trail of water on the floor. Carlo gave them a little bow with his head as he moved himself next to me.

'Hello.' all three women said. They didn't seem bothered by our appearance.

'What were you doing out here? It is pouring outside. You two must be freezing.' one of the women said.

'Oh, I am fine.' I answered. Carlo on the other hand wasn't as fine. My hand had been shaking, but Carlo was shaking all over.

'Where are you from?' another woman asked.

'We are from Italy.' I said as I turned to Carlo. The rather creepy smile had returned on his face. 'Please forgive him, he doesn't speak French.' I said. Carlo nodded.

'Don't worry about that! What brings you here?' one asked. I had waited to tell them why I was here. It had felt a little weird to start with that. Maybe it was just the place that put me off.

'Do you know where we can find Rosalie?' I asked. Two of the women looked at the one in the middle. She suddenly looked a lot less comfortable.

'That is me.' she said softly. Like she was scared the other two would hear. I had found her. Now that I had, I had no idea what to say. I didn't even know if she knew Servius. She was the only person that could help us further.

'Did you know Servius?' I asked. Her eyes flickered with panic, but she calmed herself down before she spoke. It gave me hope that she did know him. She was going to be able to tell me who Servius was.

'Fransisco?' she asked. She couldn't hide the surprise in her voice. Carlo shifted. He had noticed something was going on.

'You know me?' I asked.

'Let's go somewhere private to talk.' she said. Rosalie turned around walking off to the other side of the church. She waved at me to follow her. 'Yes. I know you. I sent you off with Servius when you were little. He had warned me that one day you would come back. I just hadn't expected it so soon.' she said.

'Soon?' I asked. Quite a bit of years had passed since I had last been here.

'Yes. Well no. I don't know. I hadn't expected it all to be true. I had expected Servius to come back.' she said, clearly in distress.

'He died.' I spit out.

'Oh.' she whispered. She seemed rather sad, like she had really known him.

'You knew him well?' I asked. She looked up, her eyes were watery.

'Yes. I used to serve him. I helped him with his whole escape. Almost got myself killed. But it was for a good cause. But now that he is dead. Things will change.' Rosalie said. I had no idea what she was talking about.

'What escape?' I asked. She looked up surprised.

'He didn't tell you?' Rosalie said.

'No. He didn't talk much about his past. I hoped that you could answer that mystery for me.' I said. Rosalie looked behind me. I turned around to see that Carlo was still standing near the other two women. He had been given something to dry himself off with, but it didn't help much. Carlo looked rather uncomfortable.

'Let's go outside. It is not a good idea to let them hear.' Rosalie said. She nodded to the other women. They were both looking at us. Eager to get even the least of information of what we were talking about. I waved to Carlo that he should follow me. I didn't know if he understood, but I didn't care. I was completely focused on following Rosalie. To get to know who Servius really was. I followed her outside into the rain. We both pulled our cloaks a little tighter as we walked past the graves. She walked over to a specific grave. The grave of King Louis the 16th. We stood there for a while. Both staring at the grave. I waited for her to speak.

'Meet Servius.' Rosalie said. Raising her hand to the height of the roof, that hung over the grave.

'This can't be. Servius isn't buried here, he can't be Louis the 16th.' I sputtered out. She turned to look at me. A pitied look in her eyes. I hated it. 'Don't look at me like that. I don't want your pity.' I said.

'Of course this isn't Servius. His body is buried where it is buried.' Rosalie said. She lowered her arm.

'He was burned.' I said. The words seemed crooked coming out of my mouth. I had burned him. Rosalie nodded.

'He was burned where he was burned. But Servius was Louis the 16th. This is going to be a long story. I will give you all the details you need. Do you want to get somewhere out of the rain?' she asked. She looked rather cold, but I didn't want to waste any more time.

'No. This will do.' I said. Rosalie nodded, clearly not happy to stay in the rain. But she did not complain.

'Louis the 16th had been a beloved king for most of his life. But it couldn't last. It is most uncommon for kings to rule until their death. Louis was destined to die at the guillotine. Together with his wife. They would be executed together. We didn't want the king to die. We loved him. He was truly a great king. He knew how to be a leader. So we made for the execution to be postponed. We were given three days. We made a plan. Servius would be changed by someone who looked like him. She said pointing to the grave. I didn't know him personally. I don't even know his name. God, I am awful. But I did it for a good cause. We made sure that the fake king wasn't allowed to say something during the time of his execution. That would have surely given away that he wasn't the true king. All went well. We were able to sneak the king out. Servius was safe. We tried to do the same with Marie. But we got caught.' Rosalie said. She spoke slowly, scared that I wouldn't understand all that was being said.

'Marie?' I asked.

'Marie Antoinette. His wife.' Rosalie said, pointing to the grave that lay next to the king's. There she was. The person whom I had been trying to find during this entire journey. I could stop here. Stop her from telling me the entire story. I already knew who he was. Maybe the time to stop had passed. 'She got caught when we tried to sneak her out. So this is the real queen. That is where you came in the plan. Your father helped keep Louis safe while sneaking him out of the country. If they travelled with a kid they were less likely to be asked any questions. You traveled along with Louis. Your father followed a day behind. Meeting you in Rome. There you were sent to stay with someone.' Rosalie said. That someone that been Carlo. I didn't know if he had followed us outside, but I couldn't get my eyes to look away from the grave. 'They figured out the rest of the plan there. I wasn't involved in that part. I later got informed that you made it safe and sound to an island. And that he had changed his name to Servius. So that was who I needed to address my letters to. Maybe you can tell me where he has been. I have been worried about you. Only got a letter once in a while telling me he was still alive. But that stopped a few years ago.' Rosalie said. I met her gaze. She looked hopeful at me to clear all that up for her. She was sharing her story with me. I felt like I could only do the same.

'He became a plague doctor. He worked on Poveglia. Our home. A little island between Venice and Lido. It is, or rather was, a place where people who had the plague were sent to. To keep them away from the rest of the world. On Poveglia we would try to cure them. But not one of them survived. My father died there a good while back. The plague got him. Servius kept teaching me. Italian, French, Latin, and astrology. I grew up. Became a doctor just like him. Always by his side. Then he too got the plague.' I said. My voice broke. Not for my father but for Servius. The man that I had looked up to. The man that I believed to have known. But I didn't. 'He died not long after. I burned his body. He told me to get his ring and ashes to his wife.' I said. My gaze went back to the grave of Marie. A person whom I had never met, but had been so important to me.

'I don't think he wanted you to bring his ashes to his wife.' Rosalie started. 'I think he wanted you to deliver a message. We had a plan. For after. Louis would take over Napoleon's place. He would get back on the throne. But now that plan can no longer be achieved. We will have to take plan B. I think that is what he wanted you to do. And you succeeded.' Rosalie said. She stopped for a moment. Her eyes lingered on me. 'He is proud of you.' She added. I didn't take that well.

'Why did he do this? He sent me away. He didn't even tell me the name of his wife! He didn't tell me where to go. He let me figure it all out by myself! He left me!' I said. Tears were streaming down my face. Not that it was noticeable with the heavy rain.

'He wanted to keep you safe.' Rosalie began softly. Taking a step towards me, holding onto my arm. 'Not everyone here is over his death yet. It would have been dangerous for you if he had told you who he was. There had been talk that he wasn't the one to be executed. We haven't been able to keep all of it down. Even if you hadn't believed him, it would be dangerous to walk around with that information. He didn't mean to leave you. If his death were in his hands he would have made sure to die after you. The letters he did send me were often long. Bragging about how good you were doing. Telling me about all kinds of fun you two had. How much he cared about you.' Rosalie said. She tried to look me in the eyes but I avoided her gaze. I wouldn't want to believe it. Any of it. Servius wasn't the one to let someone else die just so he could live. Maybe that wasn't who Servius was. That was who Louis was. Perhaps he felt bad about it. Trying to make things right by working on Poveglia. Me being part of his mercy play. She let go of my arm and we stood there in the rain for a while. I took the gourd out of my cloak. I wasn't sure if she knew anything about it, but it was the only loose end.

'The wooden gourd!' Rosalie exclaimed. I took out the bloody handkerchief and held it up in my hand. The sleeve of my cloak fell down, exposing the skin of my arm. The heavy rain was pouring down on the handkerchief. The water was mixing itself with the blood, running down my arm in small streams.

'Whose blood is this?' I asked.

'Marie's.' Rosalie answered. Something in me shifted. I had been so scared that it had been Servius's blood. But it hadn't been. 'Not every one that helped with the plan was happy about how things went. Louis left before his wife did. Him being the main priority. When he got angry at us about his wife he was given this. I don't know who gave it to him.' Rosalie answered.

'Maximilien Robespierre.' I said.

'Oh.' She replied. I knew there was nothing that needed to be added to it. I put the handkerchief back in the gourd. The red blood painted the inside. 'Do you have any questions?' Rosalie asked.

'No.' I replied. She took a few steps away from me.

'Okay. Now that I know he is dead I will have to tell the team the plans have changed. Do you want to work with us?' Rosalie asked. There was no part of me that wanted to help with whatever they were going to do.

'No.' I managed to say.

'Okay. Well, if you have any questions you can find me inside.' Rosalie said. She gave me a little pat on the shoulder as she walked off to the church. I stepped over to the grave of Marie, so that I stood in front of it. This was it. I kneeled down on the ground. The water had already soaked my pants and I didn't notice the wet ground. I took the bottle with the ashes out of my cloak. I didn't want to leave the whole bottle there, in case anyone would take it. I opened the bottle. The rain quickly found its way inside and began to fill the bottle. I didn't let it get far. I spread the ashes on the grave. Leaving nothing but a pinch behind. I closed the bottle, leaving the pinch there. I needed it. That was the part of Servius that I was familiar with. I took off my glove. The inside was moist and cold. I slid the ring off my finger. I took one more good look at it. I didn't feel bad about leaving it behind. I dug a little hole in the grave, just big enough for an entire finger to fit in. I pushed the ring down into the dirt. Covering it back up, like nothing was hidden there. I patted the soil down and stood up. The ash that I had spread had already mostly been taken away by the rain. My hand was covered in dirt as I put my glove back on. Carlo had moved himself next to me. He looked even more soaked than I did, telling me he had been standing outside this entire time. I forced a small smile at him before I looked back down.

'Will you translate that for me?' Carlo asked.

EPILOGUE

It was in the middle of the summer when the little boat hit the side of Poveglia. Carlo held onto the island, preventing the boat from floating away. It had been an extremely hot day. We both had left our cloaks at home. splashing some of the water on our arms to cool us down.

'Do you want me to go with you?' Carlo asked. I looked at the island in front of me.

'No. I won't be long.' I said. I stood up in the little boat. Dragging myself onto the island.

'Take as long as you need.' Carlo said to me, handing the bottle over to me. The bottle was a little lighter now it didn't hold Servius's ashes.

'Thank you.' I replied. I turned around and walked onto the island. Mosquitoes were swarming all around me. I tried to hit them away with my hands, but there was no use. It hadn't truly been that long since I had last been here. But it felt like I had entered a completely different world. The plants had grown quite a bit, taking over the sides of some of the buildings.

The buildings that were towered into the sky. Seeming bigger than they ever had before. Looming over me, waiting for me to get stuck in their trap. Never to be released again. I wondered if Servius ever felt this way. Knowing the world around it holds just as much if not more beauty than Poveglia did. Poveglia did seem a little less beautiful, a little more cautionary, now that I had seen the world around it. But it was still home.

It was good to know what was around you. No surprises, just the things you had always known. The good and the bad that you could count on. The ordinary and daily rhythm. There was still a little bit in me that longed to stay here until the end of my days. Knowing that it would never be like before. It wouldn't hold the same comfort, the same feeling of being secure. The image of home would slowly fall apart the longer I was here.

That was why I wanted to make it quick. To keep most of those feelings intact. The memories that I have of this place are now still whole. Each single one of them wonderful and never-ending. Even though I would never be able to experience those feelings in the moment, right now, I would still be able to look back at them. Get a tiny flicker of that feeling that would be forever in my heart. I wouldn't want to lose that.

I went over to the edge of the water. Where Servius and I had fought. Where I had thrown a doctor in the water. But above all, where Servius and I had swam. I couldn't think of a happier moment with him. This was the Servius that I wanted to remember. This was the last memory that I wanted to hold of him.

Each time I thought of Servius, after getting to know everything about him, I forced my mind back to this memory. Trying to rewrite Servius in my brain to someone I wanted him to be. I single memory that held everything important about him. So to never forget the things that are most important.

I turned around the bottle in my hands. The glass reflecting the sun. This was going to be the end. I had talked a lot about this with Carlo. Deciding whether or not to go back. To see Poveglia once more. But I decided to visit one last time. Truly knowing, and understanding that after this I would never come back again. I wanted to leave this part of my life behind me. Physically, at least. I knew that I wouldn't be able to do that without a proper goodbye.

I kneeled down on the edge. There was still a pinch of ash left in the bottle. I looked at Servius. I dug my hand into the dirt of the island. Taking as much in my hand as possible. Spilling some on myself as I began to fill the bottle. I pushed as much dirt in it as I possibly could.

When no more dirt fit in the bottle I closed it off for the last time. I dipped the bottle into the water. Holding onto it for a little longer. Taking one last good look at it. Once the image was burned into my brain I let go of the bottle. It started to sink to the bottom of the sea. I kept watching it until it was swallowed by the darkness. Preventing myself from coming back here to save Servius. To get him back to me.

The sea ahead of me was filled with ships. Life had started back up again. Like everything that had happened here was simply a dream. Nightmare to most. Shoved away, never to be thought of again.

I stared at the ground while walking back to Carlo. Not wanting to feel the gloomy buildings towering over me. Not wanting a different image of home. Carlo still sat in the boat, holding onto the edge of the island, though the water was the most peaceful it had ever been.

www.ingramcontent.com/pod-product-compliance
Lightning Source LLC
Chambersburg PA
CBHW020233030726
47497CB00009B/3077